WOUNDED

WOUNDED

a novel

— by —

Jason McCord

First Edition
May, 2024

ISBN: 979-8-9861139-6-8 (Hardcover), 979-8-9861139-7-5 (Trade)

Library of Congress Cataloging–in–Publication Data is available upon request.

Published in the United States by Malediction,
an imprint of AEA Press, LLC.
aeapress.com

For my Dad,

who instilled in me my love of books, horror, and westerns,

in that order

A NOISELESS patient spider,
I mark'd where on a little promontory it stood isolated,
Mark'd how to explore the vacant vast surrounding,
It launch'd forth filament, filament, filament, out of itself,
Ever unreeling them, ever tirelessly speeding them.

And you O my soul where you stand,
Surrounded, detached, in measureless oceans of space,
Ceaselessly musing, venturing, throwing, seeking the spheres to
        connect them,
Till the bridge you will need be form'd, til the ductile anchor
        hold,
Till the gossamer thread you fling catch somewhere, O my soul.

—WALT WHITMAN

1868

THE ARIZONA TERRITORY

JANUARY 4, 1882

There appeared to be four robbers. Sloppy, and poorly armed, by the look of them, not one of them holding a rifle or shotgun. Their leader, a vaquero in ragged boots and a patched overcoat, let his pistol hang low at his side. His three bandits, ambling behind him a few feet, were lazily slouched over their horses, tired or drunk, and probably cold. A wind, gusting, bitter and piercing, came from the north, keeping them bundled. They were rough, like their misguided leader, probably fresh from the territory to make their fortunes. They had not yet learned that rough and capable were not the same.

The edge of town was clearly in sight, just beyond the bushwhackers, camped on the coach line. The air was clear and bright, and even through the bouts of wind, the leader's call could be heard clearly, even from within the stage. "You heard me, now get out the strong box. Watches, your money." His voice was hard, with a mixed accent, but he lacked conviction in his tone; in his experience, it usually did not take much. The whip had not moved from the box, as he had been told to do, and the carry–all did not have a conductor, moving fast on its way from Flagstaff. Nobody moved.

These kinds of robberies were becoming common-place, with the recent increase in goods coming in more frequently, following the railroad being built west.

"I ain't askin'," the leader growled, his attitude souring quickly. His pistol raised now, aiming at the driver. The arm wavered loosely, his gun large and heavy; his inex-perience was clear. When still nobody moved, the bandit leader seemed to start to lose his nerve. His small posse were clearly becoming concerned. "Who's in there? Throw out your weapons!" the leader bellowed, desperate. The wind gusted and the driver shivered. The driver gave a swift kick to the boot under his seat.

The door to the stage, on the right, opened like a shot and Lieutenant Jonathon Harris emerged swiftly, dressed in his crisp blue coat, and it was this sudden flash of bright wool that seemed to startle the would–be thieves. He moved easily and carefully, allowing the weight of his outstretched arm to carry him around the edge of the open door.

He landed easily and cleanly onto the ground, firing quickly. This shot spooked the horses, causing them to turn the bandits away. On the lieutenant's second shot, the leader fell to the dirt like a dropped sack. The others, startled and slow, could not recover. These bandits were used to settlers, cattlemen, and other easy marks, and this had made them soft, careless. The other door of the coach opened and a Pinkerton agent, a man named Barnett, stepped out, clutching a Sharp repeater. Harris and Barnett fired several shots between them, and within a moment, the last robber had dropped, clutching his side, all thoughts of harm passed.

The steam from their mouths and the smoke of the gunpowder made a sour taste on the air and it was eerie quiet. The clouds above were heavy and getting dark, threatening something bad to come, but the wind had not yet moved past the occasional gust. The smooth plains of the high desert were quiet and dry, only a slight shiver in the dead grass.

Harris meticulously reloaded his pistol, an ivory handled Single Action Army, and approached the fallen thief, who was muttering to himself in broken Spanish, trying in vain to hold the blood into his leaking gut. Harris knelt down beside him, resting on his knee, slipping his Colt back into its holster. Harris picked up the thief's pistol, a poorly maintained Schofield, full of rust and dirt; Harris doubted to himself the iron would have fired straight more than once.

"You boys come from Mexico?" Harris asked, fixing the man a strong stare. He tossed the bandit's gun off into the brush, as he would not need it any longer.

"Nogales." The vaguero's voice was shook and wet, he was bleeding in. It would not be long now.

Harris took him at a half–breed, based on his skin and accent, probably just up from the Rio Grande, maybe his father had been one of them boys during the skirmishes at the border and got himself a Mexican wife. It was known to happen, and many of them were now working the cattle ranches along the border. Ranching obviously was not exciting enough for this one.

"You got a name?" Harris' voice was calm and detached as he looked over the man. The wind blew again, increasing his discomfort.

"*Por favor*," the thief begged. "Whiskey."

Harris looked over his shoulder to the reignsman and called for whiskey. "I'll get you the whiskey. Your name."

"Valdez." His voice was wavering, weakening, and he was fighting.

"Well, Valdez, you got a gut shot," Harris answered simply, handing over the whiskey the whip brought. Valdez took a gulp and winced. "You're going to die. I'll get you a

Christian burial, here in town."

Valdez just groaned in response.

"Any more of you, Valdez?" Harris asked, staring hard at the dying man. When Valdez did not immediately answer, Harris lightly slapped the side of his face. "Valdez, I need to know. Are there are more in your gang?"

"No, no more." Valdez could barely be heard.

Barnett approached, still cradling his Sharp rifle.

"Anything else, lieutenant?" Barnett said, refusing to look to Valdez. Barnett, a lifelong champion of law and order, despised such men and looked down on them, as a rule.

Harris nodded, resettling his hat, a crisp tan wide brim, but kept his place, watching. He waited a moment, watching Valdez take a few more ragged breaths. The bandito's hand slipped and with a final push, his chest stopped moving, the steam of his breath dwindling. Harris, satisfied, swiftly stood and walked back to the coach.

"Should we gather them?" the whip asked.

"No," Harris said harshly. "Leave them, we have a schedule to keep."

II

Despite what he had been told, this camp was nothing like Harris had expected. While he had seen some railroad work camps in his time, this one was something else. A road, of sorts, had been allowed for, mostly for coaches and some horses, it seemed, widening and narrowing wildly as it went, carpeted in the fine powder dirt of this area. On either side, a seemingly unending sea of white, tan, and brown canvas tents littered the area.

The encampment more or less followed a north–south orientation, with the rail line being built at the southern end, running east to west, some of the tents coming up within a few feet of the gravel bed of the tracks. Everywhere, people loitered about, moving from place to place, the air thick with the smoke of hundreds of fires and countless personal meals, mixed with the unmistakable smell of horse shit.

As the coached pushed further into the town, a few larger tents came into view, some of them quite extensive. Harris immediately thought of the hospital tents they had set up in some of their larger battles in the war. One he recognized as a mess tent, given the streams of workers and the thick white smoke coming out the back.

In the heart of the town, as it got closer to the tracks, he was surprised to find more large tents with a sort of wooden facade put in front of them, giving them a more permanent look like the shops found in larger towns. He was sure a strong enough wind could topple most of them, but it did give a pretty good look and would fool a fool or a drunk.

It was late morning when the coach stopped at the

shotgun structure that served as the Atlantic and Pacific Railroad office, a hastily assembled narrow wood structure, barely even six feet wide. Harris stepped out with a sweeping sense of self importance, flanked by Barnett and another man named Ahlborn, Pinkerton guards assigned by the railroad to protect Harris from the lawless nature of the unsettled Arizona territory. While Barnett had been a long serving lawman, Ahlborn had earned himself a reputation for predicting, and busting, some of the union stalwarts in Pennsylvania years before; he was here to make sure there were not any labor conflicts.

"Mr. Barnett, could you get the payroll please?"

Barnett, flanked closely by Ahlborn with his hand on his pistol, grabbed a strongbox from the carriage. As he was coming with security, Harris had agreed to bring their monthly payroll from the railroad office, for just what happened earlier that morning with the bandits. The driver busied himself with the luggage while Harris took in the town. For a place that did not exist prior to a few weeks ago, Harris was impressed.

Outside of the larger tents that housed the many enterprises that made up this town, the personal tents that littered the ground varied wildly, many of them forming miniature camps among themselves, much like the soldiers did in the war, each surrounding a fire of some kind, some with a cooking pot. Nearly every day a new pup tent would spring up, joining the other slapdash camps. The smell was something to behold, Harris noted, a mixture he had not experienced since his time in Virginia with the Second Massachusetts Cavalry.

Harris turned back to the office to see a lank man walking quickly down the muddy lane. Harris knew this must be a man named Brooks, who had been the A&P foreman, up to this point, a man of high regard. He was a sinewy man, with a shrewd face, which had been beaten into a fine leather; he had been leading the construction for the past eighteen months, since Albuquerque.

"Mr. Harris," Brooks said, by way of greeting, as he got near.

"Lieutenant," Harris corrected. Brooks seemed to want to respond but ultimately said nothing. While not a physically imposing man of stature, Harris possessed a strong, square face with sharp, wild eyes that gave little room for argument. His demeanor carried a heavy weight to every action and word and his neatly trimmed appearance lent him immediate clout. He was a man of bearing in a world that saw it none too often.

Brooks nodded grimly and gestured Harris to the door of the office. "Welcome to the Cañon Diablo."

19

III

The office, if it could be called that, was bare and functional with roughly assembled furniture and a cot in the corner. Unlike most of the structures, tent or otherwise, this had a functioning wooden floor, made of elevated plank panels, which squeaked horribly with every step. Despite the wind not yet strong outside, Harris could clearly hear it whistling through the walls. One corner was piled, neatly, with documents and notarial books on a simple desk, all having to do with the railroad. The blueprints for the coming bridge were pinned up on the wall.

Harris had seen worse.

"So, Mr. Brooks, what can you tell me of this… town."

Brooks smiled grimly, busying himself with throwing some wood into a stove about halfway down the wall. Harris was happy to see a stove, given the cold. Half a chord of it was stacked as high as it dared in the corner near the stove. While he had experienced cold many times, at this altitude it seemed to bite right to his bones. He missed Missouri, as odd as he found that thought.

"I ain't much of a mister," Brooks answered, his voice measured, "and this ain't much of what you'd call a town. Just a busy damn stage coach stop, though it got better with the whores gettin' here, settles 'em down. Bad news to have folk just sittin' and drinking."

Harris listened, looking out the door onto the street, as was his way. He found staring at folks while they talked to him unsettling. Despite the cold and threatening weather, he was surprised to see the number of people moving, with seeming purpose, up and down the lane.

"Has there been violence?" Harris asked.

Brooks grunted thoughtfully and lit his tinder, throwing it carefully to the bottom of the stove, as the fire caught, he seemed satisfied and shut the door. The heat was already being felt at the fingertip. "No more than what you would normally expect. This is a pretty well stocked camp, with the carriage line. Some drunken fights, sometimes the outlaws come in and cause trouble, but nothing we can't handle usually. We have some guards, from the railroad, but no law."

"Not even a marshal?"

Brooks shook his head. "One feller suggested it, over at the gambling hall, took a beating for it. Heard a story Marshals did come, and we was layin' him to rest at sundown, but I wouldn't put much stock in that. Folk talk, tall tales is all. No graveyard here. Sheriff sent someone around a week ago to get a bank robber, but he weren't here."

Brooks stared at Harris, who seemed lost in his own thoughts, still staring out the door, dressed in his, to Brooks' mind, ridiculous wool outfit. Plenty of things to keep you warm that don't stick out like a bruised toe.

"Is there a lot of bandits?" Harris spoke with a refined edge to his voice that did not rightly belong, having been raised in Maryland but spending the rest of his adult life moving from the Atlantic further back west, after the war; it came off as queer to those who heard it but could not figure out why it did not work.

"We got all sorts here, Lieutenant." Brooks contented himself to roll a cigarette while he spoke. "Most of the territory is settlin' down, 'specially in those silver towns. Progress. We got gamblers and some hustlers, even some of them gunmen they run out of Cochise County couple years ago, though they don' make much a fuss, unless they're cheated. Some cowmen, usually a rough but good sort. Though they're mostly passing through, some get stuck here with the poker, whiskey, and whores."

Harris seemed to find this troublesome, looking for the first time to Barnett, who had been leaning against the wall nearby, his rifle ever ready, resting on his thigh. He gave no expression.

"We will have to keep an eye." Harris cleared his throat and looked to Brooks for the first time, who met his gaze flatly. "The bridge is already on its way and we see no delays in finishing it. We are projected at six months, still, unless the snows are heavier than expected." Harris handed over the wire he had received two days prior from the railroad, back in Flagstaff.

Brooks nodded, tucking the paper into the ledger on the desk top. Brooks respected the clear ability of the lieutenant, Yankee though he likely was, but did not think him long for the territory and didn't wish to invite confidences. Men of authority did not last long here. Brooks managed to hang in the last four years as he was the one that paid the workers, kept them on task, and he never said a word to anybody. "Well, this office is yours, got it built right away, only a little ways from the tracks. Should be better than a tent, at least. The cot in the back there is new." Brooks was a worker, not a talker, and was over being the welcoming committee: he had work to do.

"I'll need to look at the work logs, but that can wait. The stone masons are done, right?"

"They are." Brooks answered, already making his way to the door. "Foundations are settled, finished them just after Christmas and the engineers been testing them. We are ready for the line."

"Well done, Mr. Brooks." Harris' tone was curt, a man incapable of cutting loose. The manner he spoke in did not invite doubt and Brooks only nodded again. "The track is on schedule to begin arriving in just under two weeks, along with some of the new builders."

Brooks pulled a book from the shelf nearest him, a thick register that he handed off to Harris. "The work crew logs. Got 'em on the west end now, just got a fresh load of ties they're puttin' down. Expectin' em back 'fore the end of the week. They're always back Friday, before nightfall."

Harris gave Brooks a half smile, which could have almost passed for embarrassment. "How's the food situation in the camp?" While he was more than a decade out of the Army, the notion of asking, or even complaining, about food made him uncomfortable. Despite any misgivings, Harris was a man who liked his meals.

Brooks pointed down the lane, toward the tent that Harris had correctly guessed to be the mess for the railroad workers. "That's the standard fair, open to all the workers. Frankly, lieutenant, its about what you would expect. Gets a little better when provisions come in fresh, and Christmas, but its a lot of hard tack and stews. Mornings are mostly oats, beans." Brooks turned his head and pointed to another tent across the street, not nearly as large, sporting one of the larger wooden facades, bearing simply 'Saloon.' Next to it, a large covered wagon was parked haphazard-like, with all manner of things scattered in front of it. "The saloon there, no real name for it, it has some of the better whiskey in the camp. Chuckwagon there has the best food, you can eat in the saloon, if you prefer. That's what I'd recommend, if you got a strong stomach."

"Strong stomach?"

Brooks grunted. "The cook is an ornery one, makes

all sorts. It tastes fine, just don't ask what it is."

Harris finally made to leave the office and he titled his hat in appreciation and was nearing the door when thinking got the best of Brooks, with; "Lieutenant!"

"Yes?"

"Ain't none of my business, but these boys, they're saddle men, most of them, and while the workers won't give a horses' ass, some of these boys in town won't like you parading around, dressed like you are, with your title. That's a union coat, ain't it?"

"The war is over," Harris replied, already annoyed with the notion. "Has been almost twenty years, now."

Brooks frowned. "Not to some of these boys. You just mind yourself, now."

Harris made to argue, then thought better of it. If he was truly in such a lawless place, as it seemed to suggest, would be to his benefit to not invite trouble. Harris nodded at the foreman. "Appreciated. Many rebs here?"

Brooks scoffed, taking a tobacco pouch of his pocket. "Ain't no rebs, lieutenant. Just folk with long memory."

Harris cracked what could be a smile, nodding in appreciation. "I want to see the town, while I can. Is there only the Main Street?"

Brooks laughed, the only real laugh he remembered having. "No Main Street here, lieutenant. They call this Hell Street."

IV

To call the muddy stretch a street was generous. The ground, mostly hard clay, nearly red in color, was mixed with a soft sand that made for poor going, even on foot. The office secured, Ahlborn had decided to go look into the barracks and other railroad operations, busying himself with his own affairs, as was his way.

Harris wanted to take in more of this town and become familiar, given the small respite before the bridge arrived, flanked closely by Barnett. Barnett had been with the Pinkerton Detective Agency since the war ended, working his way west throughout the years, engaging with the Indians along the way. He and Harris had quickly established a rapport with each other, starting in Kentucky, men cut from the same cloth of sensible justice and longing for structure in the world. Barnett had never told the lieutenant, but he found him to be the sort of man the country needed and would do anything to keep him alive. Barnett had never had the vision men like Harris did, but he recognized it all the same.

It was near midday before the sun came through the heavy clouds, warming up the air, taking the burn out of the lungs, though the wind had picked up, gusting longer and more frequently. It was only a few yards from the office door that Hell Street terminated with finality at the tracks.

Harris stayed just at the edge of the freshly packed gravel, marveling at the still gleaming rail line atop the heavy wooden ties. While not an engineer, Harris always marveled at the industry pushing the country forward, and could not be anymore pleased to be involved. He had joked that he would follow the rail all the way to the shore and when they got to the ocean, he would find a way to make trains swim.

The track continued for nearly a half mile to the west, with the tent–works of the town continuing all along the way, on both sides of the tracks, though there were fewer on the south side, away from the main camp. These tents were worse than the others he had seen, many of them barely more than rickety lean-tos over a bedroll. Harris guessed this must be where many of the undesirables stayed, or perhaps some of the poorer followers.

He dutifully followed the snaking line until they got the end, finding a worn path that had begun to form, waiting patiently for the first of the bridge elements to arrive, about a hundred feet from the edge of the canyon, leaving the rough and bare terrain to the drop.

The canyon seemed larger than it was, and though he had never seen it himself, it reminded Harris of the Grand Canyon, something seemingly impossible and vast. The canyon, where the bridge would go, was only a little over two hundred feet across, Harris would guess, but for a train it might as well be a mile. He would conquer this, as he had everything else in his life. For the first time he noticed the rims of the canyon sloped down, not the sheer drop he was expecting from such an infamously difficult crevasse. Surely, it was too steep to easily clamber down, but not an immediate death sentence to go over, should you find yourself overstepping.

Harris stared out, watching the faint movement of those beyond the canyon's western rim, laying ties and foundations to meet on the other side. He watched for quite a while, taking in the sun, and the moment. While he had worked with the railroad on a number of projects, most recently in Utah, this was one of the larger duties he had been given and would be a boon to his career.

He noted the stone pillars, recently cut and installed by their masons, jutting strongly from the ground, ready for the bridge and line on its way. Secretly, he was personally pleased to be getting so much closer to California. He had never been, and while he doubted anything of worth would be there waiting, he was determined to cross the country. From there, he could find new things to conquer. Maybe California would be everything he needed it to be. Maybe it would be enough.

Harris finally stepped away and faced Barnett. "Day's getting on. Let's get some food, we have a lot of work to do."

V

It was a decent walk back to the town, and as they got nearer, the smell of cooking food overwhelmed all else. Harris had a hardy constitution, but he struggled to keep up on his needs when traveling, and the lack of food was affecting him more than he had realized.

As they turned onto Hell Street, Harris was amazed to see even in the last hour, the road was even busier. All sorts of folks were moving hither and yon, workers, ladies, and ranch hands, by the look of some of them. Harris was surprised by the number of cattle workers in the town, but given the state of Flagstaff, he guessed their wages from the summer went further in a place like Diablo than the more established towns.

Electing not to punish himself more than he had to, he figured he would take his first meal at the chuckwagon, as Brooks had suggested. The man at the wagon–camp, if it could be called that, was a short and rail thin man, moving hastily, muttering to himself. He seemed to pay neither man any attention, throwing things into a large cauldron he had perched over a substantial fire. Harris noted, to his horror, that despite the sharp cold, the man was dressed only in grubby shirtsleeves with no coat in sight. He did not seem to notice anything odd about that.

Only as Harris and Barnett approached closely did

the cook stop and pay them any mind. His face, like something made of rough–hew tree roots, was twisted awkwardly at the jaw and Harris could notice the man had no teeth as the cook smiled broadly.

"I'm Amos. Wha-can I do ye fer?" the cook asked, as a challenge. He seemed almost confused as to his role. Before either man could answer, the cook held up two long fingers. "Ten cents, bacon and beans. Two bits for both you fellers." His accent was wild, unrestrained, marred by his disjointed jaw, making him near impossible to understand. Already, the cook pulled out some tin plates, badly beaten, dumping a slop of thick brown muck onto the plates.

"Two bits is..." Barnett started to object at the calculations but Harris cut him off, handing over the quarter dollar. The cook tossed the coin into his mouth, likely out of a habit of biting the coin, but without teeth it proved worthless. Both men dutifully took their plates, perplexed.

Once inside, the saloon was no gem, but it sufficed. Decently constructed, the building, like all in the camp, was long and narrow, with the bar running near the length to the back, where the small but busy kitchen kept going at all hours. Like the office, it boasted a raised wood floor, though it appeared to be hastily nailed wood panels set side by side with wide gaps; a misstep would break an ankle potentially. The quality of the food was reflected in its prices, keeping the grubby tent less occupied. The room smelled of roasting meat from outside and stale tobacco from within, a far sight better than the smell of the camp at large. The innkeeper, a serious looking man getting on in years, noted their entry with a nod of his head and pointed them to a free table in the corner.

Harris tucked himself into the bowl of what had been called bacon and beans by Amos the cook, but was actually a thick meat stew, elk by the taste, and it was mighty fine, though it did not look it. Neither he nor Barnett had thought themselves cold but the warm food and coffee, courtesy of the barkeep, told another story. Barnett seemed satisfied, in particular, a man known for his fondness of regular and hearty meals, when he could come by them.

Halfway into their meal, the barkeep, who introduced himself as Gentry, topped up their coffee, and Brooks entered, carrying a plate of his own. He gave a nod to Gentry and took a seat at the table with Harris. None of the men spoke, not at first, each focused on the warmth and gentle comfort of their stew. All three of the men, despite their differences, knew the gentle comfort and wisdom of enjoying a meal in peace.

"Any trouble with the Indians?" Harris asked suddenly, his grim disposition warmed by food and gentle company. The saloon had only a few patrons, all quiet thus far, and not even a poker game yet in the day to ruin the quiet. Brooks chewed thoughtfully.

"Nah, can't say. We got a tradin' post, even. Navajo. Decent folk. Farmers mostly, they don't stay long. Bars won't serve em, anyhow. They trade silver, damn fine work, really. Some pelts, good blankets. Half the beds in town got their quilts."

"That's good. We had more trouble with the Comanche out in Texas, things got bloody," Barnett chimed in. He was not overly fond of Indians, having fought many of them during and since the war, largely on the government payroll, and he made no attempt to hide his feelings. Harris kept practical concerns about the Indians, and he did not harbor the hatred men like Barnett did.

Still, Harris deferred largely to his companion regarding Indians, and he regarded Barnett a moment, chewing slow. "I agree. No need to make enemies. Any details I should know, about this town?"

Brooks finished off his stew, sitting back in his chair and sipping at the bitter but serviceable coffee. "Weird place. It's big, but it ain't a town, strictly speaking. Sinful place, we ain't even got a church, though you can bet they still want the sabbath for the rest. Runs all day and night, 'round here." Brooks took his time, rolling a cigarette thoughtfully, carefully. Harris waited patiently.

Brooks took a long drag and gathered his thoughts. "This here ain't a nice place, lieutenant. We got 'em as bad as they come, and more keep on comin'. The rustlers and gamblers, thieves and murderers, they're all but drove out of Tombstone, Prescott, and even Flagstaff. Running from law and civilized folk. So, they all been coming here on their way, though they mind themselves, don't want to ruin a good thing, I reckon. Nobody here to say no, without catching a shot. I want you to be careful and just mind the railroad, let the rest handle itself."

"What the dregs do isn't a concern of mine, least not yet. We focus on the build, we keep our workers safe." Harris knew better than to overly promise or deliver, keeping his response short.

All three man had finished eating, each thinking their thoughts, and allowed the silence to grow between them. Brooks was beginning to see why the railroad sent a man like Harris, wound tighter than a pocket-watch and just as timely. While he still had serious doubts about the long term success and safety of an authoritative man like Harris, he had the sand to get his hands dirty and that would probably serve him well, if he could stay alive.

The challenges of this assignment had given Harris some reservation, but surely not enough to stop or slow him, the lawless nature of this work camp, for as big as it might be, was still a work camp, had been understated by the railroad. He was sure it could be done, but he would have to be more careful than he originally believed.

VI

Night comes early in the winter desert. Even the lowest of the foothills outside of Flagstaff were over a mile in elevation, surrounded on all sides by steep, jagged peaks. Even by middle afternoon, the sun would begin to tilt sharply and the light went quickly, and the high mountain peaks made sunset come much faster. The desert does not hold the heat or the cold well, and without the sunlight, the temperatures dropped fast.

The carriage line heading east out of Flagstaff, the same used by the Atlantic & Pacific Railroad, was relatively clear and easy, but still too dangerous to travel at night. A turn in the road, an errant gopher hole, and travelers were in trouble.

Hugo and Francisco de Soto had been in this country for only six months and they were already tired of the traveling. They knew it was a long journey, but after arriving in New York the previous summer, they knew the cities were not where they wanted to be. The noise and filth, with the masses of people made both brothers uncomfortable. The large number of ever increasing immigrants made work difficult to find, especially for them, having only worked in fields and stables. Before they decided it was a bad idea to come to the country, they decided to head out west.

They had grown up hearing about the wild lands out

in the west, a place unlike anything in their home and the rumor was there was plenty of work out west. Their father had never been out of Spain, but he told such tales, all from memory, always to the delight of the brothers. Their father had been gone many years, but his stories remained, and had carried them through the country.

It had been slow going, especially through Kansas and Colorado, with the weather and locals proving difficult in equal measure. They had to light out of Durango only a few weeks prior. They had tried to get on the Denver Railroad, hoping to follow the work, but had been run out by some of the local workers, along with a few Mexicans and a Chinaman.

They had separated from the others shortly after leaving Colorado, heading into the Arizona territory, riding hard, pushing their horses as far as they dared, as they could not replace them. Once they were deep into the Navajo Indian Reservation, they slowed their pace and had mostly recovered.

Night was coming on fast and the brothers agreed that camp was called for. They had seen the clouds threatening them all day and as the sun continued, it was getting colder and the wind was kicking up. They had managed some decent equipment in Colorado Springs that had served them well so far in the cold high country, making camp a relative comfort for them.

Fifteen feet off the southern side of the trail, they had found a sandy patch of flat ground that would serve as a good camp site. Francisco wasted no time pulling their tent roll off his horse.

"There's no trees close by." Hugo stood just to the side, watching Francisco, contributing nothing. Since coming out of Colorado, the trees thinned and were getting harder to come by near the trail. Worse than the lack of easy firewood was Hugo's unwillingness to help.

"Maybe it don't kill you to ride off and cut us some wood, eh?" Francisco offered, throwing their packs on the ground. He loved his brother, he was the only thing he had left, but he was ready to leave him for dead in this desierto with all of his useless belly–aching.

"That's... far, huh?" Hugo responded, pointing to the nearest tree, nearly a hundred feet off. Hugo was struggling more with English than Francisco was, but they had been determined to keep to it, which made communication challenging from time to time.

"*Estupido*, go before it's too dark. It's going to be too cold tonight." Francisco was done with this and busied himself with their tent, kicking down some standing weeds, trying to flatten a spot. Hugo finally grabbed his hatchet, one of their recent purchases in Colorado Springs, and stomped off to the nearby tree. Finally with a moment's rest, Francisco savored the moment a little.

Despite his complaints, he liked this place. Nobody minded what they did here, and nobody ever asked questions, letting them travel easily, and cheaply. The only real challenge had been the cold and that dust up with the railroad in Durango, but he tried not to dwell on it.

Francisco looked at the large peak in front of him, watching the last glow of the sun light the trees that run along its outline, little more than colors at this range. He had learned just a few days prior that these mountains were called the San Francisco Peaks, which amused him immensely. It may not be his mountain, but it still bore his name.

His back and rear hurt, but it did not take away from the sight. The sun was almost entirely over the edge of the mountain, but before it fully went, a last blast of sunlight, a bright marigold, shot into the sky, hitting the dark clouds, and setting the mountain's edges ablaze. It was a hell of a way to end a day.

Hugo was not enjoying his time nearly as much as Francisco. As he chopped branches off his hundredth tree, he still could not help but wonder what so wrong with Amarillo, where they had some found decent work on a cattle ranch. Hugo had liked the place well enough, and many of the hands were from Mexico. Their Spanish was not rightly the same, but that didn't matter to him, it was better than English.

Francisco had always been the dreamer, and as the eldest, Hugo supposed he had a right to be. His idealism was not winning any favors with Hugo though. He knew California was not too far off now, and the weather, he was told, was much better. Maybe he could convince Francisco to ride out the winter, get some work and maybe find a train to finish the trip. He was sick of the cold.

He had a solid enough bundle to get a decent fire started just as the sun finished setting. Before they went to sleep, if he wanted a fire going, Francisco could get the next bundle. The wind was gusting fully now and the supposed storm was looking real enough. They had been trapped in a storm in Kansas and Hugo hated it. They should have waited in Texas.

Walking back to the camp, Hugo could hear little more than the wind in his ears but something made it through; he thought nothing of it at first. It was a high whine, something like an animal might make. Aside from horses, Hugo had yet to see many animals out in this part of the country. He stopped and listened, bracing against the irregular gusts of wind. It was there, but it did not sound close and he moved on.

Francisco had their camp up, and had wrapped himself in a blanket. Hugo stacked up the bed of the fire as quick as he could. His fingers were getting numb and stiff in the cold and he moved as fast as he could. Francisco said nothing, waiting as patiently as he could for Hugo to start he fire. Hugo had gotten pretty good at their camping fires and Francisco was content to let him continue.

There was a piercing howl, coming from the growing dark outside of their camp. It was impossibly loud, and it sounded like it came from only a few feet away, if it were not for the echo on the air. The wind killed the sound quick, but both brothers took notice.

They only had one weapon between them, a shotgun they had picked up for ten dollars, and neither brother had fired it yet. Francisco jumped to his feet, reaching into his saddle and pulling out the long gun. Both waited, their senses dulled in the dark and gusting wind.

The sound was frightening, a scream of evil. Hugo, never one for anything he could not see with both eyes, softly and carefully recited what he could remember of the Lord's prayer, his eyes darting uselessly in the dark. There had been no other sound, save from the wind in the grass, and this rang worse than any silence could.

Another sound came up, a lower, guttural growl that seemed to roll across the ground itself, seeming to follow them in a circle. It was a sound of threat and menace. Francisco pulled his younger brother closer to him, trying his best to protect him, though the open prairie made it impossible to tell where the sound came from.

Wind only again now with the cold, bitter and merciless.

Seconds of nothing stretched into painful minutes. The nerve of both men were at their breaking, as no man has the experience of monstrous evil to brace them. Carried on the wind, they heard a great rustling, as though something were tearing across the dirt at a great speed. It was unlike anything they had heard, with the speed of a horse but without the thundering impact of hooves, it sounded more like a skittering noise. By time they could tell where it was coming from, both were hit by a large force, knocking Hugo to the ground and staggering Francisco.

Only Francisco caught a glimpse of it, some loping gray shape in the dark, little more than a lighter shadow against the dark blue of the night. He aimed and fired his gun uselessly, lighting his vision and deafening him. The force of the shot startled him, making his foot further uneven, his ears filled with a shrill ringing. Only after a few seconds could he hear his brother screaming.

Hugo was on the ground, his voice a high shrill of panic and fear. Something had hold of his pants, giving it, and he, forceful tugs, like somebody had sicced a dog on him, pulling him a foot at a time, great drags, more than any dog, or man even, could manage.

Francisco readied his weapon again, but could only barely make out his brother, being pulled ever further from him, seeming without cause. Something had him, something terrible but he could not see it nor fight it. Hugo's voice faltered a moment and there was another great tug, and he slid from view entirely. His screams echoed louder, thunderous cries of anguish. It was haunting, but tolerable, until there came a new sound, a soft ripping and shredding sound, that belonged to no fabric.

Francisco was no coward, and he loved his brother dearly, but as the screams faltered, he had a decision to make. Whatever thing had his brother, it was too dark and too late to help. Francisco could stay, but he would only die himself.

Francisco dropped the gun and tore off into the other direction, clumsily climbing up onto his horse, nearly falling off the other side before righting himself. With a great cry, the desperate man gave his nag a kick and took off into the dark, hoping only for the grace of God as he left his now silent brother behind.

VII

The bitter cold air had no chance with the throngs that poured into the larger tents that made up the saloons and gambling halls mixed into the drag. Shouting, cheers, and arguments flooded out of each building, mixed with the smell of tobacco, sweat, and alcohol.

The wind kicked up with a fight after the sun went

down, driving everybody out of the street; snow was coming any moment, and it could end up being a hell of a storm by the feel of it. The shanty camps at the south end of town struggled the most, some of the clusters building larger fires to combat the cold. Some of the more enterprising were already making arrangements for taking shifts on maintaining their camp fires.

Harris finally had his office, and now room, squared away enough for his liking. The cold, which had persisted since at least Wichita back in October, was starting to wear on him. While he did not consider himself an old man as yet, he certainly was not as young as he once had been, and he wondered if that had any bearing on his reduced endurance for the cold.

Before the snows came and made things harder, he had decided to take his chance and take in the rest of the camp, mostly the camps to the north that housed the workers. Leaving the makeshift office, bundled in a heavy wool coat and his hat pulled down low, he hooked around to the rear of his shanty, walking down the back of the west side of the camp, enjoying the relative quiet. As the cold swept onto his face, he thought about allowing his usual clean shaven beard to grow, as a means of fighting the damned wind that seemed to plague these mountains. In the meantime, he would check the general store in the morning for a scarf.

As he walked, as briskly as he could manage, the last of the larger and more permanent structures ended, giving way to the makeshift camps of canvas tents. The first cluster, nicer and newer tents of a hardier material, appeared to be primarily the railroad workers, arranged neatly and into some sort of sense. In front of many of the tents, several of the workers appeared to be resting and socializing, each sitting around camp fires of varying quality.

The workers had reached the arroyo ahead of the planned bridge, giving many of them a rarely occurring respite. Some talked, sharing stories of their exploits, or loved ones they missed. One older man skillfully plucked at a guitar while his fellow campers listened. Harris was surprised to see one younger man, little more than a boy, helping a grizzled old man write a letter home. None of them paid Harris any mind.

The tents pressed on, continuing to diminish in quality and consistency as he moved further from the main heart of the camp operation. These tents, still serviceable, appeared to Harris to belong to many of the followers, those that had made a living following the railroad operations, providing whatever products and services the railroad did not, usually indulgences.

A fresh gust of wind came in off the plain and pushed Harris on his way back up the street, which proved surprisingly well lit, despite itself. A relatively large but patched and weatherstained tent appeared to be the first saloon he happened across. As he looked into the tent opening, it seemed smaller, darker, and rougher than he liked, great bellows coming from men, each the same drab brown of the desert around them. He thought it likely the cheaper citizens would go to a place such as this.

Halfway up the street, the largest non–railroad tent stood out, a saloon lit up like a Fourth of July celebration and it made an awful racket. This business sported the largest and best built of the false fronts, including a roofed porch that ran the length of it. Oil lamps hung from the porch eave and loud piano music rang out, played by somebody who knew their music. It was busy, as all the halls were, and a group of men were entering as he approached.

VIII

Garrett Lewdon fancied himself a tough man. Pushing forty with bad teeth and starting to show signs of consumption, he had originally been driven out of Texarkana some years before, in a fight over wages. He often told folks he had killed a man for calling him yellow, but the truth was such that Lewdon had fled to avoid the wrath of his former employer.

Bad luck dogged him endlessly across the desert, including the death of a confidant in a botched robbery in

New Mexico the previous year. Along the way he had gathered two men, Fred and Bill, fools to be sure, to follow him around, attracted to his jawing about his glory days. He had yet to do anything worth notoriety, but he searched still.

The braggart had stumbled onto Cañon Diablo by accident, following a supply line to what he thought was a depot he could rob. Instead, he had found the camp at its peak and instantly became attached. It was his kind of place, just large enough to slip around, but not so large as to easily hold him accountable.

He and his cohorts surveyed the place quickly. Half a dozen poker tables were crammed into the narrow space, no two of them alike, each packed with rough looking men of every shape, color, and size. The tone was loud, jovial, and comfortable. Two wood–stoves kept the room warm, despite the wind and coming cold.

There was a narrow but well stocked bar at the far side, and they pushed through the crowd, careful to not interrupt one of the games, as knocking a man's chips over might just be enough reason to shoot him down. Behind the gambling tables were a couple of small, wood tables, just big enough to set a drink on, and thankfully an empty stool at the bar.

Lewdon removed his hat, setting it on the bar. He leaned haughtily against the chipped wood topper, chuckling to himself.

"What'll it be?" a voice called out. A wide–hipped woman in a bright red dress marched over, already fixing him with a practiced, hard stare that felt like a challenge.

"Whiskey. Three," he shouted, trying to be heard over the noise.

The woman was already moving, quickly and easily, not a wasted movement. Lewdon watched with interest, thinking his private thoughts; it has been some time since he had been with a woman properly. She hastily poured the drinks and then went back to staring. Her face, round and pleasant, was at the edge of losing its battle with age, still appearing lovely, but the harshness of her life was showing its toll. While she appeared genial, her eyes showed the harshness in her.

Her steel colored eyes was enough to convince Lewdon to move his attention. Most of the folks in the saloon were sat at the crammed in tables, but a couple sat at the bar itself, by themselves. One of them was a man he had not noticed when he walked up, but now he couldn't see how. He was a bear of a man, taller than most and broad at the chest and the middle. He was seemed content to his drink, hidden behind a large and well–worn leather coat, an equally rain–stained gray hat tilted back.

"What's yer name?" Lewdon asked. He phrased it as a challenge.

The man seemed to only barely notice, taking

another drink of his own whiskey, a shot still in front of him, his mouth hidden behind an unkempt beard, dark and laced with thick chords of gray. Lewdon was immediately rattled by the man's lack of response. He slid closer, standing now to his full height, looking down at the old man.

"I talkin' to you. I asked, what's your name?" Lewdon raised his voice. His two compatriots brayed laughs like donkeys. This only spurred Lewdon further. He moved to mere inches from the man, chuckling to himself.

The woman stood in front of both of them, her face contorted into a mix of concern and contempt. "Best leave it be, Josiah," she said to the old man, who had still not moved nor showed Lewdon much attention. Lewdon laughed louder now, reaching out and taking the man's shot, and slammed it back easily.

"Oh," was all she could mutter, stepping back from the counter. The hulking man, Josiah, turned slowly on his seat, turning his attention to Lewdon for the first time. Lewdon was able to see his face fully now, deeply lined and worn into a saddle–leather toughness, making his age hard to determine exactly. His eyes, a cold and flat gray that matched his hat, were piercing and alert. Within eyes like those was only pain, violence, and death.

Josiah gave a low grumble, a sound only to himself. Lewdon misjudged the man, still laughing, turning his attention to his friends, dividing his attention, and he did not see the movement. Josiah rose in a single movement, his forehead driving forward into Lewdon's nose, knocking him off balance. Before Lewdon could recover, Josiah was on his feet, a full head taller, and nearly twice the weight.

Josiah's hands, large and as rough as his face, grabbed Lewdon by the top part of his shirt, ripping half the buttons off as his hand twisted. His right hand, an open palm, swiped quickly, bashing Lewdon across his jaw, clanking his remaining teeth together, and spilling blood.

"Wait," Lewdon tried, feebly, his voice lost. Half the saloon had stopped to watch the violence, with great enthusiasm. Lewdon's two friends had nothing to do or say just yet, shocked at this turn of fortune.

"Not a word," Josiah growled. His voice was deep, and seemed to echo in his own chest, with a strong dip of sound at the end, as if out of breath. Lewdon said nothing, largely due to his confused state, his head swimming, swaying on his neck loosely. "You took my drink," Josiah said, an admonishment.

"I didn't—" Lewdon tried. At a surprising speed, the back of Josiah's hand knocked into Lewdon's right jaw, knocking his head the other way violently.

"You don't listen well," Josiah said evenly. His tone had not risen or fallen in the slightest to this point. Josiah carefully reached out and took a hold of Lewdon's unclaimed whiskey, locking eyes with the thug and drinking it methodically. His eyes never blinked. Once the whiskey was finished, Josiah set the glass down and finally released Lewdon, who stumbled back into his friends. "Now, get out."

The saloon patrons, watching with great intent now, waited carefully, sensing a tipping point. Blood dripped freely from Lewdon's mouth and nose, his eyes glassed and watering. Josiah turned back to the bar, settling his large frame onto his seat with a grunt. One of Lewdon's fellows, Fred, the smarter of the two, started to help him to his feet, but Lewdon shoved him off, reaching into his coat.

None of them had noticed Harris moving ever closer during the exchange, and they would not have if he had not pressed the barrel of his Colt into Lewdon's temple. Fred saw it and froze, gripping Lewdon tightly. The cold steel barrel stopped Lewdon in his tracks.

"I don't want this," Harris said carefully. "You take him outside, and you get out of town, and we let it be, boys."

"Look what he did," Lewdon said, through gritted teeth, his voice softened and broken by his injuries.

Harris sighed. "You took the man's drink and thought him a soft target. He could have killed you. It's a blessing from God, son. You boys, gather him up. I want you gone." The finality in Harris' tone ended the conversation.

With a great heave, the two grabbed Lewdon under his arms and hauled him from the saloon. The patrons gave a mixed reaction, laughing at the fools now being run out, but most disappointed at the lack of more bloodshed. By the time the three cleared the doors, everybody had returned to their games and drinks.

Once they were truly gone, Harris holstered his pistol and turned to his attention back to the bar. The woman behind the bar walked back his way, and Harris noted her tucking a shotgun back under the bar.

"Well, you need a drink," she said simply. Her face had not softened.

"Coffee," Harris said simply, standing to the counter. She nodded and he watched her pour from a tin coffee pot on the stove behind her.

As she sat the coffee down, her eyes narrowed in a challenge. "You the new boss?"

Harris winced at the awful coffee and set a coin down on the counter, which the woman immediately snatched up. "I am," he finally answered. "Lieutenant Jonathan Harris." The coffee burned and tasted like copper, but he said nothing.

"Brooks said you came in," she replied. Harris thought her face might be loosening up but he could not be sure. "That man can gossip like an old hen. I am Abigail." Her tone was matter of fact and Harris was not sure he heard her right.

"This your place?" Harris asked, sipping the awful coffee.

Abigail cocked one of her ample hips and scoffed. "Honey, they're all my place. Where do you think all those places came from out there? I was one of the first, half of the rest came from my people going off. This camp was even worse before we put some decency in the place."

"Well, happy to hear it," Harris said, smiling. He already liked her immensely.

She nodded gravely. "Course you do. You just gonna have coffee? I can get you one of my girls to comfort you, if you like." She indicated broadly to the many girls standing around the floor. Harris shook his head, which made her laugh heartily.

"Abigail," Josiah said suddenly, his voice the same even tone. "His next drink is on me." Harris turned in mild surprise, meeting eyes with Josiah, who could only shrug. "You saved me some trouble there. Least I could do."

Neither man looked away. There was no challenge in either look, and neither man knew what to make of the other at first. In each, a history could be read, and the mettle of the man could be seen in its full measure. The look on Josiah could only from the war, and Harris guessed which side a man like Josiah fought on.

Neither man spoke, both sizing up the other. The numerous deep cut lines of Josiah's face shifted into a pained and awkward frown of amusement. Harris doubted the man could smile.

"Ogden," the grizzled veteran finally offered, giving a curt nod. "Josiah Ogden."

"Harris. Lieutenant."

Josiah let out a booming, barking laugh, his shoulders heaving with the effort. It caught a couple tables attention for a moment.

"Lieutenant," Josiah answered, a simple acknowledgment. There was a hint of amusement in his response, and Harris took it in stride.

Harris felt a bead of sweat despite the bitter cold. He was sure he could skin and out–draw the grizzled drunk, should it comes to that now, but he could have friends and he may not escape the violence. Josiah shrugged and turned his body, facing Harris properly. "Don't you worry, Lieutenant. Any business there might be between us was done a long time ago. Ain't that so?" Josiah's face remained open, earnest, and even; only those eyes held the violence that worried Harris.

"It seems so," Harris says eventually, and he felt his body loosen up. "You're awfully far from home, aren't you?"

"As are you, Lieutenant. Feller's gotta live somewhere, don't he?" Josiah considered a moment, clearing his throat.

Harris said nothing for a moment. "Yes, I suppose he does."

Josiah leaned back on his stool and Harris heard it

creak. While he was certainly growing a belly, he was not a fat man, possessing a large frame and thick arms, visibly wrought in muscle. In his prime, he was probably nearly three hundred pounds. Age had diminished him from the monster he must have been in his physical prime.

"Have a seat, Lieutenant. I ain't gonna bite," Josiah offered. His tone was as hard and clipped as ever, but there was an earnest note to his voice. Harris took the offered seat carefully, trying to keep himself loose. He had encountered his share of rebs from the war, and while none of them had gone to violence, he had not encountered them this far on the frontier.

"What brings a man like you to work for the railroad?" Josiah asked. It was something Harris had heard many times before, and would likely hear again. There was something different in the way Josiah asked. Most folk, when they asked, were asking about the nature of his work, but Josiah seemed to be asking about the nature of the man.

"I knew the fighting could not continue forever. Even during the heaviest fighting, I knew the only hope lied in the future, after the bloodshed was done. I knew we would win. Eventually. After the war, I served with the Third Military District, helping with Reconstruction. While there, I saw that the railroads were bringing that future that I saw. Goods from Boston to Atlanta in days, not weeks. Imagine what that could bring. After my discharge, I took a job with

Union Pacific."

Josiah did not immediately answer, seeming to consider, staring at his drink. "I have seen what it brings, Lieutenant. First hand. Everything is moving, sure, just like you say. We will keep building, expanding. Towns like these will come up, and then go again. Just a fast. Maybe we find gold along the way. Someday, that we will never see, the whole country will be filled up. Every spot found, and named. Everything built. And then?"

Harris stared hard, and there was a long pause. Neither man said anything for quite a moment, both patient for an answer that most assuredly did not exist. Harris took a pained drink of his coffee. When Harris finally spoke, his voice was resolute and like a preacher might: "Years ago, when I was in Texas. I was working for a cattle ranch. I found a book, one of the few they had. In it, a man, can't rightly remember his name, but I'll never forget, he called it 'manifest destiny.'"

Josiah said nothing, allowing Harris to speak freely. After a beat, he continued.

"I had words to tell me what I had known, even during the war. It is by God's will, we are to expand and settle. To better the world by showing a better way, to lead by example. Industries, the railroads, the liberation of the negroes, defeating the indians. We are going to build a better world. We are going to do it better." He paused a moment, catching his breath a moment. He had not noticed that his voice had risen. "I will see to it."

Josiah seemed satisfied, nodding to himself, and fully turned to Harris, fixing him with a hard stare. His eyes were flat in color but hiding behind them, there was a wild desperation, a haunted question that was still left unasked. "You have luck out there, Lieutenant. I will be curious how things go for you here." Harris knew by his tone that their conversation was over. He did not think Josiah wished him any harm, though he was sure the reb would not shed a tear over his death, should that happen.

With a nod, Harris turned and let himself out of the bar, his coffee left half finished on the counter. Abigail watched Harris go with mild concern, this exchange making her doubt the fragile polite peace that existed in town. Josiah, for his part, did nothing for a moment and then resumed drinking his whiskey. Abigail gave him a hard look. "Should I be worried, Josiah?" He looked at her, but his rough and chipped face made reading his expression hard, and then he grunted humorlessly.

"No need, Abigail. We had our time, but that was a long time ago. We saw the same thing in each other, is all. Gettin' a sense."

Abigail cocked an eyebrow. She had not known Josiah long, only learning his family name that very moment, but they had formed something of a kinship. Most men who came into the camp wanted something, whether it was work, a fight, drink, or someone like Abigail. She had turned down several proposals in the past year, since she started following the camp. So far, Josiah did not seem to want anything Abigail could figure, least of all her, and that already put the man at the top of her list.

Abigail waited but the veteran had nothing to add. In the month that he had been there, that was already more than Abigail had ever heard from him at once. She excused herself and Josiah made no sign he noticed.

Josiah looked in the mirror behind the bar, watching the growing crowd behind him. It was busier than usual, and Josiah could only imagine the knowledge of the railroad advancing, work presuming, and the added security for the payroll helped improve morale and get the workers out of their tents and bunkhouses. The storm would likely stall things for a week, maybe two, and he reckoned this would be the last major shindy for a while.

Josiah Ogden tried not to bother himself with the affairs of the town, and none seemed to want anything to do with him. Despite the inherently violent nature of the man, he had no interest in harming another man and harm is all he had found in this burg. He had a life riddled with it since leaving North Carolina, and he wanted to be rid of the town as soon as he could. He was not sure, really, where he would go, same as it had been for the past ten years. He was almost to the west coast, a place he had never seen, nor really cared for, but it was different, at least.

Josiah's thoughts were interrupted by shouting and yelling from behind. A couple of the railroad workers, joined by a couple drifting cowpunches, were looking out the front of the saloon doors, to a loud fight happening in the street. There was a rapid scraping of chairs as the hall cleared, people pouring outside, pursuing the fighting men. Abigail approached Josiah, watching the door like a hawk, upset at the fickle attention of her clientele. Josiah stood, and stretched, his aging back cracking with the strain.

IX

By time Josiah made his way to the porch, three men were fighting wildly in the street in front of a different saloon on the other side of the street. After a moment, his eyes adjusting, Josiah noticed it was Lewdon and his two friends. It seemed that Lewdon was not ready to beat town and decided to establish himself once again.

A crowd had formed quickly, but not too closely. A quick left hook knocked Fred onto the ground, to the cheers and approval of the throng. Bill took a swing, but he was as drunk as Lewdon, and clearly never taught to fight. The punch did not connect. Lewdon, despite not being the outlaw he thought he was, was a harder man, and the fight turned bloody, fast.

Bill, a strong and able man of notable height, stood little chance against the dirty punches from the outlaw, who was jabbing with underhanded punches to the Bill's ribs. Excess whiskey kept both fighting longer than they ought to have, each of their faces now busted, broken, and bloody. Lewdon's own face was barely recognizable any more.

Within a moment, the fallen Fred got to his feet and both stood before the outlaw, now winded, and out of his depth. "You ruttin' bastard!" Fred shouted, wiping blood from a split lip. The outlaw said nothing, but his hand was on his gun, still in his holster; Bill, the sharper of the two stumbled back in alarm, falling to the ground hard. The scene stopped, and time froze, and for a moment, nothing stirred.

It was an unspoken rule of engagement, scuttles such as these were handled like men, and the last man standing won. There was no law in this camp, nothing official, but the armed security provided by the railroad was usually enough to keep things from getting too bloody. The drunk outlaw clearly had decided he would not be playing fair.

Bill, having found new mettle, sloppily scampered to his feet. He was slow and clumsy, and before he could find his feet the outlaw had drawn and fired. The sound of the shot echoed quick and hard and caused all to flinch and draw back. Bill fell back and curled into a ball and made no more movement. The outlaw turned to fire on Fred, helpless and confused, his hands raised in feeble defiance. For a moment, all thoughts of harm had gone.

Josiah's shot from the porch was fast and true, neither seen nor expected, hitting the outlaw Lewdon clear in the chest, tearing a hole in his chest, dropping him instantly. The whole exchange took only a moment and the sound of the shot rang for a time while the crowd immediately dispersed, particularly among the workers, as fighting was not tolerated and could lead to dismissal.

From his view on the porch, Josiah could only holster his pistol, frown and shake his head. He had watched the whole thing with a stiff indifference, knowing how this would play out the moment he saw the type of man fighting. It always amazed and disgusted him how quickly the crowds formed and went away, always watching. These gawkers, yellow–bellied fools who thought they knew what death was, what it meant. They flirted with it in these displays and they always lost out in the bargain.

Fred was pale as a ghost, seated in the dirt, looking to his dead friend. It was a look Josiah knew, just as he knew nothing would ever make it go away. A steady stream of the crowd made their way past Josiah, back into the bar. They disgusted him, the lot of them, and everybody like them. Abigail followed up the rear of the chain, her face screwed into a hard scowl.

"Y'all pay your tabs, or you can join them fellers in the street!" Her bite was no slouch, but it was her bark that ran blood cold in that town. Abigail waited for the last of the men to get inside before her face relaxed and she looked to Josiah. "Why'd you save that boy?"

"I didn't save nobody. That curr would have turned on me next, or some other fool. I had a shot and he needed killed." His voice was flat, but Abigail easily picked out the sadness.

"You seem a might more interested than ya should, not knowing them. Surely somebody else would have stopped him," she observed. Her language belied her appearance, the lack of polish and a roughness to her words that came from a life around camps like these. Hearing her speak pleased Josiah, he only wished she had no need to speak this way. He knew whatever was in store for Abigail was not anything good, he only wished to never see whatever it ends up being.

"It's just stupid, Abigail," he finally answered. "A waste. Life weren't always so cheap, was it? I'd like to think so. This is the 'progress' our lieutenant loves so much? What's changed?" As he spoke, Josiah saw Harris approach the dead, now being attended to by a couple townsfolk and the undertaker, another necessity of the railroad, especially given the cholera. Harris was talking quietly with the people around and Josiah watched carefully. "Maybe it was this cheap, this easy, and always was. We were just too busy to notice. I reckon I won't know for sure." He turned to look at Abigail, her face full of confusion and worry. "It doesn't matter, never you mind me. I'm tired."

In the street, the bodies were dragged away, careless, like chord wood. Blood darkened the rocks and sand of the road where those boys fell.

"Come in for a drink," Abigail offered. "I may even let you not pay." Abigail was known to refuse free drinks to the good lord Himself.

"I think I've had enough for a day like this." His usual gravel of a voice was softer, disjointed, the clipped ending more pronounced. For the first time, he looked wearier than Abigail had ever seen him. With a tip of his hat, Josiah stepped slowly off the porch, looking both ways of the street, filling his lungs with the air, watching the few folk walk from one side to the other. The air was getting colder and the storm was here.

Josiah tried not to linger on his thoughts and turned to his camp. Like many, he had set up a pitched tent on the southern end of town, surrounded mostly by the railroad workers. He had found a good spot far enough off Hell Street, where most of the surrounding tents were filled with the negroes and sojourners, since the railroad would not pay for their lodging. Josiah found them pleasant and quiet company and they all let each other be. He never understood the attitude toward such men, they were good enough folk, honest and hard–working by his estimation.

Josiah's walk was slow and contemplative, despite the growing cold and wind. As the larger building and tents cleared and made way to the beginning of the tents, the night got quieter and the air was still. Josiah caught faint smells of cooking meals, dirt, mud, blood, and shit. Similar smells to his time in the camps during the war, and he found it almost comforting. Something one would never think to get used to, even coming from farming in the eastern foot-hills, but life was funny like that sometimes.

"Look at that!" Josiah heard a voice off to his right and did not take him long to see why. Coming up, near center of Hell Street, was a lone gray wolf, trotting at a strong pace, seeming to go nowhere in particular, braced against the wind. Josiah stopped in his tracks and watched. The wolf never broke stride and seemed to pay little attention to anything in particular, its head and eyes darting left and right frantically. Josiah noted that it looked ragged, as if it had been running for a time.

The wolf was not deviating, its pace unbroken, headed straight for Josiah. He drew his pistol, a heavy and well worn Colt Dragoon, still smelling strongly of gunpowder, but he did not aim it yet, knowing a lone wolf to be of no particular threat. But the wolf kept advancing, and Josiah knew better than to turn his back to it. With twenty feet to go, Josiah raised his pistol but another shot, from off to his left, stopped him. The noise of the gunshot was loud, a rifle.

The wolf's body jerked to its right, landing with a final and sudden thud into the ground, dying before it even knew what happened. Josiah did not move, keeping his gun leveled at the fallen wolf. A single man, rifle in hand, came from the camps on the side of the street. Josiah holstered his pistol as both men approached.

"Ain't that an odd sight," the young man said, tucking his rifle around his shoulder. Josiah said nothing, kneeling next to the dead wolf. "It's no pup," the young man continued, "should know better. Looks lean." The man seemed to be talking more to himself.

Josiah looked right at him. "I appreciate the shot."

The young man chuckled. "You didn't shoot. Looked like you choked. Wasn't that, were it?" Josiah shook his head slowly, still looking at the dead wolf. The young man continued speaking; "Call me Moon. Momma called me Thomas." Moon offered his hand.

Josiah gripped it, tightly. "Josiah." Josiah said nothing for a moment, staring at the dead wolf. "It was alone." He did not easily invite confidences, but something about this young man rang true to Josiah.

"Still, it was after you," Moon offered, shivering now in the cold.

Josiah shook his head slowly. "It wasn't coming for

me. I was just in the way. It was just running. Away, from something. Without a pack. This is all damned odd."

"Yep," Moon agreed, now hunched over the wolf and turning its body to look at its injury.

"When have you ever known a Mexican gray wolf to be alone? Why would it come into town like this?" Josiah, asked, more to himself. For ten years, he had been his sole confidant and grew accustomed to answering himself. "What could scare a wolf into running into a town like this?"

Moon shook his head, confused. "No way of knowing. Hell of a thing. Maybe it was sick, lost its pack. Maybe looking for water. Not much around here, especially this time of year." He said nothing for a moment, looking over the fallen animal. "Well, I'll take the wolf, tradin' post will want the pelt, meat can be sold. Unless...?" Moon trailed off, studying Josiah's face, but the old man just shoot his head. Moon's mouth split into a wide grin. "Much obliged. And next time, just shoot the damn thing, mister."

THE ARIZONA
TERRITORY

JANUARY 5, 1882

The temperature hung below zero, and it only seemed to get worse in the predawn hours. The snow storm had stalled overnight, but it was not going anywhere, though thankfully the wind had died down to a breeze from the gusting the previous day. In one of the newer camps at the northern edge of town, just set up in the past week, some fiddlehead had let the fire go all but out and it was near unbearable. Walter Elwein would have given anything to avoid getting out of his bedroll, he felt near death at the cold, but the salted venison and chili from the nearby camp was tearing up his guts.

The former Wichita rancher shivered and chattered as he forced on his boots and wrapped himself as much as he could, as fast as his stiff fingers could allow. As he slipped on his boots, a size too small, he noted that he may end up losing a toe before this was all over. His stomach turned and boiled and his time was short. The outhouse was near a hundred feet, at best, and it was not an easy walk, especially in the cold.

Out of his tent, Walter did not even bother with his lantern, it would take too much time. He could only think and complain in his head about being in this miserable bitch of a territory. He missed his home, and his cattle, and the regular meals of beef and potatoes. He had not had proper food going on a year and it made him miserable. This mush they had been eating could hardly be called real food, by Walter's estimation, just the sort of slop you ate on drives to keep from starving.

A loud shout and breaking glass came from down Hell Street, likely a thrown bottle, and Walter picked up the pace. He hated the rowdiness of this town and the violence, but he had to go where the work was. His cattle ranch was gone, swallowed up by all those larger considerations, and they did not want the older work hands like Walter. He was nearing forty and his back just was not what it once was.

Walter made it to the outhouse, none too close for comfort, and he was grateful to be out of the wind, even if it was on a shit–hole. Surely by the time the bridge was built, he would have enough money he could finish on his way to California, maybe even to San Francisco. He had heard there was gold and more work than a feller could handle there. Maybe he could even be a clerk, give his back a break. Might find himself a wife. Would that not be a fine way to wind down such a life as his?

Walter figured the sun would be up within an hour, he reckoned he would still be able to get warm in his bed for a couple hours before he had to be up again. Spring could not come fast enough and Walter was ready to be rid of the cold.

He left the outhouse as fast as he could, ready to be back in that tent of his for any kind of warmth he could manage; being wrapped up cold in his tent was better than out in the open. Hell, if he was lucky, maybe one of them other boys around their camp had built back up the fire, he could get even warmer.

Clearing the outhouse quickly, his dreams were crushed as he saw his camp, and the fire was barely more than embers. Peckerheads. He would have to have words with them. Even the chinaman that they let sleep in their camp, he should know better by now. Damned sons–a–bitches. Walter's mood was soured and he doubted anything would much help improve it today.

As he crossed halfway into Hell Street, he noticed the air quiet and he swore he heard something, like a scuffle. Among the noise coming from the hard drinkers still going in town, there was something else. Out in the wild, like this town was, he had heard all manner of animals, but this was different. He shook.

Against his best judgment, his curiosity got the better of him and he stopped in the street, wrapping the Navajo blanket tighter around his shoulders. The cold bit at him through his wool underwear and he knew he had to move on. But that sound, it was getting louder and closer. Raspy and vicious, it reminded him of a wolf dying of thirst he had seen out in Texas, a sort of desperate pant behind sharp teeth. He could see nothing, but that sound was not in his mind, it was coming, and definitely coming for him.

Walter picked up his feet and ran as quick as he could manage back toward his tent, the river rock and loose sand of the street making his passing slow and dangerous, especially in loose boots. He did not think a mountain lion would come this far out of the foothills, but if it was desperate enough, Walter would be in trouble. The noise was behind him now, and it was getting louder. Walter dropped his blanket and hauled out from the road, his ankle twisting and giving, dropping him into the powdery dirt.

He could hear the rustle of something coming up on him, but he would not look. If it was a wolf, the best he could hope for was to make it to his tent and make it too hard for them to get after him.

He almost cleared the road before something grabbed

the back of his collar.

He gave a short yelp of panic and was pulled straight onto his back, knocking the wind from his lungs. Lights flashed in his eyes and he could not see, gasping for breath, disoriented. He felt himself lifted off the ground, his toes scraping the ground. He had not been hoisted like this since he was a boy, and with this gasping breaths it left him at a loss to help himself. His head swam and his world spun on a top, his breath still catching in short gasps and fits, each one painful. He was dropped to the ground again, his eyesight completely failing him now, the cold the only thing he could feel in his lungs, hampered by broken ribs.

Within moments, something had hold of him, tussling him, tearing at his clothes and skin. He could not feel the pain, only the pulling sensation, and he feebly fought back against the unseen attacker. Whatever it was, he could not see it, but it was large and strong, stronger than any man. He was finally able to take in a quick, pained breath. He managed to get his first and only scream out when he felt the teeth tear into his neck and he felt the warmth pour down his chest. He stopped screaming and never screamed again.

II

Elijah Gill, a young drifter making his way from

Alabama that had a tent in the same camp as Walter, heard what could only be a scream, loud and clear. There was lots of noises made by the people in this town, but a full grown man screaming was not a normal thing to hear, especially pre-dawn. The cold air bit at his lungs and face, but Eli was never known as a coward, and he had not planned to start now. He had a rarely used double–barrel that he kept with him, and he figured he should bring that. Many of the white men in town gave him sour looks, but so far nobody had said word one to him about it. He tugged on his boots and stepped out into the dark morning.

As he cleared the tent flap, it took his eyes some time to adjust. The scream had stopped to be replaced by a loud and dwindling splash of something wet on the stones. Silence quickly followed.

He did not see anything immediately, but as he stepped closer to the street, within moments, he saw a dark pool on the rocks, visible even without light. The smell of blood came on him thick and heavy and it made him gag, a strong scent of bitter copper.

Another cowboy was coming down the road, likely also having heard the scream. The cowboy, named Garrett, was startled to see the shotgun, but Eli quickly put up his hands.

"Hold up!" Eli said quickly, motioning to the puddle. "I don't know what's done, but I ain't the one done it."

Garrett the cowboy looked drunk and confused, but he managed a nod, but did nothing further. Even drunk, it was clear that a shot man does not up and vanish. It only took a few moments before more came, one or two at a time, curious and bored, more than not. With work halted for the moment, a lot of folks schedules were upturned and the camp entertained at all hours.

Eli looked to Garrett, trying to steel his nerve. "We should tell somebody," Eli said. Garrett nodded stupidly, but thankfully another man had taken the advice and was already running up the street toward the rail office.

Eli was dumb–stricken, turning back to the obvious remains of somebody. "Where's the goddamn body?" he said to nobody in particular.

III

"There's been a problem."

Harris was awake but moving slow, his body protesting against the sharp and brutal cold. He was just putting on his boots when Barnett stepped in, already in his usual attire, without his hat and only half shaved. His words barely rattled Harris, who only shook his head in confusion.

"Isn't there always?" Harris asked, an attempt at humor, as he stood and put on his coat.

Barnett shook his head mournfully, his unusually disheveled appearance giving him a ragged look. "This is different, boss. Something… strange."

Harris went from annoyed to curious as he grabbed his coat and went following Barnett out of his office, wrapping his arms around himself to brace from the cold. While his office sleeping quarters were far from warm, his stove provided a relief from the harshest of the cold and he still had not yet adjusted.

His hat firmly on his head, Harris followed Barnett as quick as he could, relieved to see Barnett holding his Sharp rifle, as Harris had left his pistol in the office. A crowd, of sorts, was beginning to form at the end of the street, and a hysteria seemed to be growing from them.

The crowds parted as Barnett and Harris approached, all murmuring to each other. Barnett indicated Eli, who was in much the same place he started, though somebody had mercifully brought his coat.

"You see what happened?" Harris asked Eli, trying his best to soften his voice. The boy was clearly shaken and he could not handle any hysterics. Eli pointed his gun to the congealing puddle of blood in the street. His hands did not seem to want to let go of his shotgun, clutching to white knuckle. Harris noticed that Barnett's own rifle was not far from the boy's direction, just in case.

"I don' know. I heard screamin', the most awful

sound. It was a man, sure 'nough. I came out to see what happened, thought maybe was somethin' wrong. I seen this." He pointed again at the blood and would not stop looking at it. Harris thought, stepping closer to the blood, pulling his coat tighter around him. The first light was threatening the horizon and it was a bitch of a cold morning.

The blood smelled awful, something he was all too familiar with, and he tried to stomach his disgust. He saw the blood puddled a little further, with a few spots and what looked like some drag marks. "What's your name, son?" Harris asked Eli, without looking to him.

"Elijah. I don't work on the line, really, you wouldn't know me." Harris looked to him with a strong stare, amused slightly by his answer; it was subtle. Harris nodded and rose from his crouch, keeping his coat tight around him.

"You work for me now. You got yourself a horse?"

"Yessir," Eli answered quickly, trying to stop his body from shaking.

"Get yourself dressed, and I want you to find where this goes. You do that?"

"Yessir!"

"Good." Harris approached the boy and gave him a quick appraisal. Whether the boy succeeded in anything or not, it was worth the reputation to send him off, to show his charge of this town. "Take that shotgun, we're looking for wolves, more likely than not. Drug him off." Eli nodded, but did not move yet. His eyes were still on the puddle.

"Wolves did that?" Eli asked. He did a good job keeping his voice level, but Harris heard the tension.

Harris pretended he had not heard the question. "Find his body, son. He needs a Christian burial, doesn't he?" Harris gently placed a hand on the boy's shoulder and they finally locked eyes. Few white men had looked Eli in the eye like that, and certainly no boss like this man here. Eli nodded, a little more sure. "Get dressed. I'm counting on you." Eli was off, as fast as he could manage.

IV

Josiah was reasonably comfortable, the heavy gray wool coat bought in El Paso two years prior serving well against the mountain cold. He liked to set out early, having never been one to miss out on good daylight, raised on a farm like he was. It was a habit that only seemed to be getting stronger in his advancing years.

He was surprised to see as many in the town streets as he did, the cold and drink put most of them down around now. He gave his horse a kick and its pace quickened, its breath shooting clouds around in the cold air. While he made it a policy not to involve himself in the goings-on of the degenerates in this town, his curiosity sometimes got the better of him.

The first ray of light started shining out of the summit of the distant mountains, far to the east, and Josiah felt it warm his shoulders and face as he road north to the open edge of town, the buildings making way to the camps and the light clutter of passerby. Even from twenty paces, he recognized the coat and hat of Lieutenant Harris.

He really did not hold the animosity for the man he thought he ought to, but he felt it best to avoid the Yankee as much as he could. Pulling that thread could only result in trouble, and he had enough to last him a couple lifetimes; for some, the bitterness ran deep and without reason. Still, he figured seeing what got the lieutenant out of bed at this hour could not hurt. As he slowed his horse, he could hear Harris' loud and clear voice.

"Set two men down here, at the edge of the camps, make sure they have rifles. See if some fencing can be placed around the edges here, just behind the tents, keep them from coming in from the side. The rest of you, you go about your business, we won't have the rail delayed. One of you clean this up." Harris was talking to a couple of the railroad folk, and they all nodded along to every word. Harris saw Josiah, who was watching absently from his horse, but made no mention of him. Harris pulled in another worker, this one a broad negro that looked as strong as an ox.

Josiah was more than a little shocked to see him address him just like any man. Yankee or not, men of his ilk were not usually too kind to other types of folk, looked down on them mostly. "Get down to the hardware store, see if they can get us some chicken wire for fencing. He can get me the bill, the railroad will cover it." The worker took off in a hurry. With that, Harris disengaged and the small gathering had nothing to keep their attention and in the cold like they were. Warmer beds called for them. Harris waited until had moved off, save for Barnett, who had stayed, eyeing Josiah.

"Somethin' happen, lieutenant?" Josiah asked. His tone was cordial as anything, even polite. It caught Harris off guard, who had taken a quiet stance of bracing himself when talking to the grizzled veteran.

"More wolves, it looks like. Heard one was shot last night."

Josiah nodded, looking to where Harris was pointing to a dark spot on the street. "Wolves, huh?" Josiah asked. "Anybody see them?"

"I don't think so. Sent a man who heard it, see if he could find the body." Harris stared at the old man, who only appeared to half hear him.

"Wolves don't seem likely to me, lieutenant. I reckon a full grown man wouldn't interest wolves, and they couldn't have dragged him off like that. Not with this many around, any rate."

"What else then? No man did this," Harris replied,

frowning. He did not know what his angle was and that made him uneasy.

"No, weren't a man." Josiah's voice came as a rumble, trailing off in his usual manner, lost in thought. "Where's the rest? Wolves would have made a bigger mess." The last sentence was not directed at Harris, more like a muse to himself. Harris watched Josiah's horse amble closer to the puddle, the horse's head shaking when it started to smell the blood.

"Wolves or a cougar. It was too early for a cougar," Harris answered, trying to keep his handle on the exchange. Harris was no fool, and he liked to think his former enemy was neither. He knew of no other threat in the territory who could do something to a full grown man, let alone make off with his body. If Ogden had an idea, Harris would have to hear him out.

"Perhaps so," Josiah allowed, his face seemed to crack as he frowned, his heavy brow nearly concealing his eyes. Harris knew he was not convinced but thought better than to press. It was all speculation, at this rate, and Harris had better things to do, the day getting on like it was. "Did I hear about fencing?" Josiah finally said, addressing Harris with a tone that could have been a challenge.

"I did. Around the tents. Make it harder for them to get into the camps, if there's any more of them out there."

Josiah said nothing for a moment, seeming content

to watch the sun continue to rise. He tipped his hat back and fixed a look to the lieutenant he did not much like. Harris could feel all the years of Josiah in his stare, the kind of look you only see from a haunted man. Josiah could not be more than ten years older than Harris himself, but something in his demeanor gave an impression of a man beyond his years. "This is damn odd, lieutenant."

"That it is."

"Things being what they are, you are as close to in charge around here as anybody may be. I trust you will not take this lightly, a man like you. You'll keep these people safe, I'm sure."

Harris' brow rose in surprise. He would never have thought to receive something as close to a compliment from a man like Josiah Ogden. "I'll do just that," Harris replied, his face locked as best as he could. This was perhaps the strangest conversation he had had in some time.

Josiah finally nodded, seeming to be content with their talk. As he led the horse away he took one last look to Harris. "Be the man I hope you to be, lieutenant." With that, Josiah was trotting down the street and on his way out of town.

Barnett kept his eyes fixed on the departing Josiah. Ever the suspicious man, he had been uncomfortable with the men talking the last couple minutes and he was still expecting trouble. "Everything alright, lieutenant?"

Barnett asked. Harris nodded grimly.

"Find me four more guns," Harris said. "We're going to get some more posts for the next couple days, at least. We still have a couple weeks until the bridge gets here."

"We have the men to spare. I'll find them."

Harris nodded. "Don't take any from the storehouses or guarding the line, use men from the camps." He trailed off, lost in thought.

"Lieutenant? You alright?"

Harris said nothing, watching the same sunrise Josiah had. "I'm fine. See to it."

V

The northern edge of town ended abruptly, opening up to a wide open plain of chaparral and rocky prairie in all directions. Further to the northwest, the looming mountain peak was clearly visible in the distance, snow capped and omnipresent, glowing a strong orange in the rising sun. The day was mercifully free of a strong wind and the air remained clear, for now. The weather in these parts was notoriously fickle and unpredictable.

Josiah had nearly passed beyond sight of the edge of town when he heard a holler from behind him. To his surprise, the young man who called himself Moon was riding up, bundled tightly with a long rifle over his back.

Josiah decided to wait for him to catch up. He did not like the idea of somebody coming up behind him, no matter their temperment.

Moon looked sharp as he rode up, showing an experience and grit exceeding his youthful appearance. The boy could not have been much more than twenty, by Josiah's guess. "Heading out?" Moon asked as he approached, his grin wide.

"That I am. See what there is to be seen before I head out. What brings you out so early?"

"I don't sleep much, and dawn is a good time for hunting. I was already out earlier, but I needed some more bait."

The two carried on, both rightly guessing that peace and quiet was more welcome than not at this hour of the day. The glow of the sun was lighting yellow on the mountain as it cleared the horizon and shone bright, causing both men to feel the warmth on their back. The hovering clouds, which had lightly broken up overnight was gathering back, threatening harsher weather by the end of the day. Such was the weather in this country.

The town was out of sight before Moon spook up again. "Might I be askin' what that was back in town? Another feller get shot? I saw the business of it on my way out."

"No," Josiah responded grimly. He was already troubled by the events, what little he knew of them, and while he could not blame the boy's curiosity, he wished he might find another use for it. "Animal attack. Drug off one of them workers."

Moon looked incredulous. "Drug him off? What in the hell could do that? Cougar wouldn'a come into town like that, less it was starving."

Josiah nodded. His eyes looked out into an open vista, with the edges of a thick pine forest coming into detail. He had been looking for open enough land at the edge of this forest, something with enough room to plant and timber to fell. It was never a real plan, really, some idle thought tickling him here and there, if he was ever able to settle down.

As riding companions went, Moon was one of the better Josiah had encountered. Josiah always liked hunters, they tended to keep quiet unless something needed saying. Moon seemed content with Josiah as well, scouting for his hunt, giving the veteran little consideration in the moment.

In the growing quiet, the day started in real earnest and the sun had cleared the horizon, bringing some small warmth, but with it came a slight breeze that neither man much cared for. The only word spoken for nearly an hour was by Moon, turning them to the south a might to stay upwind. Though Josiah would scarcely admit this to anyone, he reckoned his days of long riding were probably close to behind him and he enjoyed these moments, taking advantage before he settled down and hung up his saddle;

his body was not able to take it like it once could.

The noise Moon made was quiet but Josiah knew immediately to wait. Both horses were well-traveled and trained and, for a time, the world was still. Josiah could see out the corner of his eye that Moon had slid off his rifle, a well—worn and clean Model 1866, by the looks of it. He was impressed by the young man's precision and deft hands as he shouldered the rifle, pointing to nothing Josiah dared to search for. A beat and a shot, and it was finished.

Moon took off quickly after his prey, while Josiah took his time to follow. The air was clear and as they neared the trees to the southwest, he could start smelling the pine, a hearty and rewarding scent that he could get accustomed to. Nothing in South Carolina had smelled nearly as powerful to him, nothing had felt nearly this peaceful. The drama of that railroad stop did not trouble him, as he knew it would vanish as quickly as it came, and only a few poor souls would ever recall it.

The hunter rode back at a quick trot, a substantial cotton—tail in his grip. He was grinning from ear to ear.

"Why you smilin' like a jackass?" Josiah asked, confused, and a little tickled by Moon's behavior. Surely he had shot any number of rabbits in his life.

"It was a damn good shot," he replied simply. Moon looked over one shoulder, than the other. "I see a clearing that way, just at the edge of the trees. Breakfast?"

VI

The sunlight helped a might with the cold but that was not saying much. Harris' first day did not start easy and it did not look like it would be lightening up. The weather troubled him, but not nearly as much as this attack. The violence of the night before was one thing, such things happen from time to time, but this random attack was a greater concern, largely because of its uncertainty.

Animals were not unheard of, but this was something else. Though it would never reach his ears, Harris was certain whispers would start soon. It did not take long for a wolf sighting, followed by a drug off man, to encourage rumors and superstitions, supplied and encouraged by the followers, hocking their wares with any story to ensure the sale.

As ordered, fencing, if it could be called that, was starting to go up around the northern edge of the town, the newest and most open part of the town. He had been surprised to see some of the drifters even pitching in to help, maybe even just to slip and grab a meal for their trouble, which Harris found an agreeable arrangement.

Work was proceeding steadily as a man rode up quickly, recklessly; it was Elijah. He was not a good rider, and struggled with getting off his mount. A frustrated Harris grabbed the reigns, steadying the nag enough for

Elijah to climb down.

"Did you find him?" Harris asked plainly, keeping an eye on the progress of the fencing posts getting driven into the ground, with some measure of difficulty. Elijah was panting and seemed haunted.

"I did." The young traveler's voice was shaken. "I… think."

Harris turned gravely, giving Elijah his full attention. "You think?"

Elijah choked down his emotion, clearly troubled. "I just found a mess, boss. Such a… bloody mess."

Harris said nothing a moment, continuing to stare. He had no words. He suddenly felt tired. "Thank you. Get some rest."

"I want to help," Elijah said instantly. Harris could only smile.

"After you get some sleep, come back and help with them with the fence." Elijah nodded dutifully and stepped back toward his camp without another word.

As the fencing went up, he was beginning to see what Josiah had been so incredulous about. While fencing made a sort of sense, the layout and random nature of the camps made it nearly impossible to do a whole lot of help; it would take weeks to properly encircle the camp, as spread out as it was, and how it continued to grow. Harris estimated a couple thousand now made up the camp.

He had little to do at that exact moment except to watch and think. While the fencing may not be all that effective to protect the town, it could help with the mindset in town, and keep down panic. Panic, this far out, could sink them. So, for now, he would ensure progress looked to be happening, if nothing else.

He noted Brooks coming from the north end of town, moving with a purpose toward him. The foreman looked even more grim than yesterday and gave a half nod by way of greeting to Harris.

"Fencing is going up, though I don't know how much good it'll do, really."

Harris nodded gravely, shuffling his feet. "I agree. How's the supply?"

"Not a lot. Mostly have it for the livery and some of the livestock we keep over yonder," he pointed off to the east, "but it's not a lot. We will be out by end of the day, I reckon."

"I understand. We can't let anybody worry. Any chance of getting a word out to the railroad?"

Brooks spit. "We don't have a telegram, nearest is in Flagstaff. Be a hard trip in this coming storm. I wouldn't try it." Brooks indicated the darkening and gathering clouds; by mid–day, they would block out the sun and the snow would come soon after. Harris finally answered simply: "We will do what we can."

VII

Given the cold, both men elected for a slightly larger fire, choosing comfort over discretion, as neither felt any particular danger here at the edge of the world. Among many things Josiah had learned in his time with the army, one he retained better than most, was the ability to quickly build a fire. Within a few moments, a stable fire was crackling, and with the burning of the pine branches, that cedar smell suited Josiah just fine. While Josiah sat at the edge of the fire, idly fueling the flames, Moon took to dressing the rabbit.

Josiah found his mind drifting. This spot could work. He had never quite figured out why he spent so much time looking for a spot to build himself a cabin. He had probably passed over a dozen potential sights from Tulsa to this mountain. He figured he was still looking for something, but never being the type to dwell on his intentions, he was ill prepared to handle that sort of train of thought. Josiah was an intensely clever man, honed by years of experience, but he lived in the moment and on instinct, and introspection did not suit him. He told himself that before Diablo up and vanished, he would have to make a choice, as just another town would make him drift forever.

"Can I ask you somethin'?" Moon asked suddenly, snapping Josiah from his thoughts.

"What's on your mind?" Josiah asked, fishing his tobacco and rolling papers from his coat pocket.

"It seemed to me you know this new guy in town, Lieutenant Harris."

Josiah did not answer straight away, filling his paper and rolling carefully. He hated to drop too much tobacco. Moon seemed content to wait, pulling the skin from their meal. Only once the cigarette was lit by a match did Josiah respond.

"I never met him before. I couldn't tell you the name of anybody who fought on that side. I just know the type." Josiah hoped this satisfied and took another draw on his tobacco.

"I weren't born yet, but I can tell who fought by lookin' at folk."

"Can you?" Josiah asked, amused. He leaned back on his elbow, smoking contentedly. The wind stayed mercifully minimal, but the weather was certainly not far from turning.

"There's a look, a sort of feel. Some folk, like that Lieutenant Harris, seem to kind of be about their time and never really let it go. And I could tell you didn't fight for the Union." Moon kept an even tone and it was clear he was only giving his opinions and meant nothing by it.

"No, I did not," Josiah said simply, his voice his usual low growl, his face without expression. "Men like Lieutenant

Harris, and there are more like him than not, saw the war as a duty. Somethin' they did because it was what they should do. Maybe called to do, though I doubt that be the case for Harris. He probably fancied himself some kind of knight, taking up arms to protect king and country, somethin' he was told in a story as a boy. Not to say he mostly doesn't do a good job of that, given the railroad brought him out here."

Moon seemed satisfied, saying nothing further as he expertly skewered the rabbit and hung it over the fire, propping the roasting spit up, but like any good hunter, he kept an eye on the pink meat. He seemed to have thoughts of his own, based on the look he had, but Josiah was not going to prod. He seemed to find the younger men struggled hearing about the veterans of the war, on either side, like they had missed out of something. Maybe it was some kind of shame, losing their daddies, and not being able to help.

The rabbit started to smell just fine to Josiah as he finished his cigarette, careful to stomp out the fire. As Moon turned the spit, the fire cracked, and the wind stayed down. Both men were quiet a long while, smelling roasted rabbit, before Josiah found himself speaking.

"I served on a regimen with Patrick Cleburne, out of Arkansas, since we were Yell Rifles together. We were sent to Tennessee, for the Heartland Offensive."

He took some time here, gathering his thoughts. He

forced a less grim tone. "I enjoyed my time in that town we were in. It had nice people, supported the cause, and we were welcomed. They entertained us, the month of December. A lovely woman named Imogeen, in particular, made the best fried chicken I ever had. A wonderful woman. That area wasn't all that easy to defend, but we had the idea that we weren't going to give up any part of Tennessee to the Union. As I recall, there were some great cedar groves in that area. Maybe that's why I like this forest so much. I haven't thought about those trees in many years. We joined up with General Bragg and we became the Army of Tennessee, and we took up in Murfreesboro."

Moon nodded, tearing a piece off of the rabbit and chewing thoughtfully. Moon had never much of schooling, helping his mother around their house, but he had been blessed with a natural perception that his mother fostered with great care, giving the young man a strong sense of awareness. He knew it best to let the grizzled man speak at his own course.

"Just a few days in, President Jefferson Davis came in person and had Bragg send thousands of men to Vicksburg. We were with General Smith, originally, but he went to Virginia and we stayed, with Hardee." Josiah took a moment here, cutting himself a piece of the rabbit, sitting up. Every bite was made with purpose, his eyes darting left to right, clearly organizing his thoughts. Moon said nothing.

"We had a quiet Christmas, at least, though that didn't help the cold. Wasn't cold like this, but it was plenty miserable. Cleburne helped. The men liked him, and so did I. Always did. We were in camp for damn near a month before the Union even arrived, I'm told. I didn' see them right away. The cavalry had those early clashes, and things got bloody, fast. Them boys tore the Union apart in that first day." More careful eating, and the world was content to let the quiet happen. The clouds were the only movement, gathering and threatening the sun.

"We were pretty evenly matched, it looked like. The situation got tense, fast. That night was a long, and cold, one. I was on the north end, on a hill. I could see the yankees down below, they were in a flat hollow, made it easy to see them all, except for the all the trees. When the attack we expected didn't happen, we were moved to the left flank that night. Now, something funny happened." Here, Josiah gave what could have been a smile, but it was the queerest sort of smile Moon had ever seen.

"It was the damndest thing I ever saw in that war. We were all camped real close to each other, only a few hundred yards, I'd reckon. It was dark and we knew there'd be no fight until the morning. As we moved to the west flank, we heard the music from the other side. Wasn't too bad, if it weren't for their songs. Funny enough, our boys started playing our songs back. Them boys, they got particularly loud about playing Dixie. It was a nice ease of tensions, I think."

Josiah rolled another cigarette, moving deliberately and carefully. Moon saw his lips move quietly, as if recounting the story to himself first.

"I don't remember who started it, us or them, but one of them boys started playing a song... can't remember which. Whatever disagreement may have been happening stopped then and there and both sides sang. Imagine it, if you can. Thousands of men, boys, really. Cold, tired, and scared, ain't one of them wouldn't rather be anywhere else, but that one song made both sides, in that moment, one people. That's something. I couldn't rightly tell you what it is, exactly, but that's as close to magic as ever I saw. If only that magic could have stopped everything." A deep sigh.

"Cleburne told us that attacking first was going to be what mattered. So, we did. It was dawn, couldn't rightly see yet, but we knew the Union would attack at first proper light, and we were going to be first. I don't remember every detail. Don't care to. I am getting old and things fade. But I remember them boys on the other side, they hadn't even finished their breakfast yet."

Josiah sat up proper now, sitting on his ankles, looking at the fire he continued to feed small branches into. It popped happily. "We had done the same at Shiloh, but it still caught them off guard. I was on the rear, behind another division. They went too far, that first division, but we closed up. We attacked all at once, one big push. I had been in dozens of fights to that point, and after, but that… that was closer to a massacre. We just went right through them. They barely put up a fight. Couldn't really, could they?

"All morning, we pushed them further back, for miles. They fought hard, but it wasn't enough. If the Union hadn't been so resolved, we would have swept the field. But their center held. Somebody in command must have had sense. I heard later that those Union boys went to the last man, but I wasn't there to see it. It wouldn't surprise me, they had sand." Sitting like this was taxing the aging Josiah so he sat back, rocking back on his palms.

"It should have been a total victory. Before mid-day, the yanks had run out of shot and we pushed. They rallied, but we could have taken the field. I found out later that Breckinridge, the man we split off of the night before, he didn't attack when he should have. We got too thinned out, and them union boys grouped closer, making it harder to get through their lines. We dug in that night and spirits were high. We lost a lot. My friend Edward died that day. We had been fighting side by side since before Shiloh. Cannonball took him right in the middle… I wasn't touched."

A swig from his water, and Josiah pressed on. Something about this seemed to need to be said. Moon was sure he was the first to hear of this. "I remember finding it odd, it was the new year and we both just stopped, all of just waiting there, taking our time. We were told to wait for the Union retreat, but a retreat didn't come. There was nothing more to be done at that point. There were too many and the weather turned. Then we got the order."

Josiah stood now, pacing restlessly. Moon looked up like a school boy. "Couldn't see a damn thing. There was cannon fire chasing us. We were lost, confused, and trying to avoid our own ditches. I had just gotten to the edge of the last treeline, and there were two Union soldiers next to a tree.

"One was near death, the other trying to dress his wound, save his life. I saw them and they saw me. It was a corporal, I think... reminds me a lot of that Lieutenant Harris. He could have killed me, he had a clear shot, I had nowhere to hide. Probably should have shot. But he didn't. If he did, his fellow soldier would probably have died. Maybe even himself. Instead, that man chose to try to save his friend and was willing to spare me to do it. He let me pass."

Josiah paced in short, looping circles. His voice dropped and became weary. "The war continued for a time, but it wasn't ever the same. The killing and dying never bothered me much before that. It was then, seeing that mean choose life, when I would have chosen death at the drop, the fight went right out of me." Josiah seemed finished, his head dropping, his voice still. But something in his bearing suggested he had more. Moon said nothing, waiting. "There are wounds in war. Some lose eyes. Legs. Scars they carry. They limp, they ache. The worst wounds aren't the ones seen."

What needed to be said had been said and both men took it in. Josiah walked off for more fuel for the fire, and Moon was left with his thoughts. The silence lasted long enough for Josiah to return with his kindling, and feed the ample campfire. The clouds had since covered the sun, letting through some light, but it would be an early night.

"I ain't never shot a man," Moon finally said, his voice low.

Josiah nodded. "Good. Plenty of killing, and how much it ever helps I can't say. I've killed men, Thomas." This caused the young hunter to look up in surprise; he had been Moon since he left the schoolhouse, and he did not think it a slip up on the old man's part. "Dozens of them. I am not likely to stop before it's all done. I have a comfort with death. Taking lives, saving them, I don't care. That comes from shootin' a man too much."

Josiah took his spot back by the fire and both men sat and ate silently, accompanied by the sounds of nature, the birds happily chirping and the wind lazily singing in the grass. Josiah finished his meal, carefully and expertly picking the meat off of the rabbit with his large knife, his eyes lost in some memory of his own.

The sun had turned in the sky and the day was getting on. Clearing his throat, Josiah straightened himself and rose to his feet, adjusting his coat and putting his hat back on. "The cause, for me, died on that battlefield. There were other battles, more death, more blood. But I lost my care for it all. Let them all hang."

Moon said nothing immediately, choosing his words carefully. He took his time tearing down their campfire and as he started burying their fire, he asked; "Why tell me all that?"

Josiah said nothing, taking his position on his horse, patting the beast's neck fondly. "You weren't there. God willing, you'll never see the like of it in your days. Maybe..." He considered. He rightly did not know what made him tell Moon about it, in this place. "There have always been wars. Men killing men. We never seem to learn. Maybe if young men like you hear about what we had to do, maybe the next will think. Violence happens, and it will keep on. It's the lack of vision, including my own. All that killing and no vision to any of it."

Moon mounted his horse, grasping the point the old man was trying to make finally.

"We best get back, it's going to be cold tonight, and if I guess right, mighty snow," Josiah said grimly. He seemed to have aged since arriving at this camp and it concerned Moon, but he said nothing, giving his horse a kick to catch up to the retreating veteran.

VIII

Josiah had been on the money about the weather, the low and heavy clouds had finally settled from the east, bringing more cold and the first of the snow, light and lazy flakes that drifted on the wind. Though it was barely evening, the clouds had shut out the majority of the sun and as the sun vanished, the wind kicked back up, a bitter and harsh cold that came from the storm. With the wind came moisture, and it made the air like shards of glass.

The last glow of daylight, a muted blue tone, showed the edge of town had changed somewhat. The north edge of town that riders came in and out of, adjacent to the canyon, now had a makeshift but serviceable fence, roughly four foot tall, made mostly of railroad ties and barbed wire, about waist high, too high for a horse to jump at a trot. It did not completely block the end, but created a sort of crescent shape that funneled the entrance into a more narrow space, about fifteen feet wide. Work seemed to have stopped for the day, likely due to the cold and wind.

Josiah, flanked closely by a bundled Moon, could freely see his breath as they came to the break in the fence. Two men, bosses from the line by the looks of them, stood bundled in layers of clothing, and topped with one of the Navajo blankets from the trading post. Each clung to Winchester rifles, standard issue from the railroad, but Josiah found the whole thing useless. In their state, they would be less than useful to fight back much more than the dark.

Moon scoffed as they cleared the two sentries, who paid them no mind. As they passed, Josiah could see one was trying to build a fire, badly. "This ain't gonna do much against a man–eater. Whatever it is," Moon said quietly.

"I reckon not. Especially if them boys are too cold and wrapped up to hold a rifle. And with all these gaps between the tents, it all seems pretty worthless." Josiah grumbled wordlessly to himself, tugging at the collar of his coat closer around his neck, desperate for a fire and some coffee. "Still, at least the good lieutenant is trying some-thin'."

IX

Giles Montgomery was a carpetbagger drunk that had stumbled into Diablo some weeks prior, right as the camp was really getting going. His initial goal was not terribly certain, he just knew he had to light out of Jeff City. An angry brother of the marshal wanted to get a hold of him after that disagreement with that young girl. By the time he had reached Colorado, he had heard enough to decide on San Francisco, much like young Elijah, taking advantage of the railroads where he could. He would get there, he was sure, eventually, might even find some of that gold rumored to be out that way. There is always opportunity for a man like Giles Montgomery.

Unlike most, Giles rather liked this little burg. It had everything he wanted in a place, including a lack of any real law. The threat of death did not concern him too much, as he kept to himself and never sought a fight while he was drinking, which was often in a place like this. The whiskey was cheap and widely available, the women receptive to most any man, especially those not covered in dirt.

This being Thursday, he had used his not-inconsiderable skill at poker to relieve some of the workers of their week's wages, usually one of the coolies, who he found pleasurable company but did not have the good sense God gave a mule when it comes to poker. It had been a couple weeks so he decided to treat himself to a cut and shave before he tucked in for a night, staying out of the cold.

The only barber in town was an ornery cuss that Giles tried to avoid wherever possible but the codger kept a clean shop and it stayed warm enough without a coat. The sun was just about set and the windows out the barber shop were showing ink-black and Giles was the last customer for that day. The barber, named Rookwell, originally out of Oklahoma, tossed Giles a towel to finish wiping up the shaving cream while he cleaned up his razor. Both men were tired and ready for their supper.

While Giles wiped off his neck, he checked himself in the silver mirror, pleased with the result. He looked almost respectable again. Perhaps along the way he would have gathered enough for a new waistcoat, might make something of himself out west, since the south was clearly no friend of his. As he dropped two bits onto the barber's counter, his mind turned to western gold fortunes and, more immediately, some warm meal across the street at the saloon.

The sun was gone now, only the most faint of a steel gray still on the horizon, behind the distant mountain and trees, fading to a deep blue fast, though many were not around to see it. Not many were out on Hell Street, some just moving from place to place, looking for warmth, dinner, and a fight, more than likely.

X

The wind had lost some of its sting with the night, but the cold was as deep as ever and would only get colder as the night went on; the snow was still falling in steady and light flakes, but as the wind caught the flakes on the moist air, it cut straight through a man's coat, burned the face.

Josiah and Moon were coming into the more established buildings on the drag, and they could hear the raucous sounds from within. Both men seemed to wordlessly agree to head to the saloon, likely for the peace and comfort of Amelia's oversight. Josiah could already taste the stew, figuring he might even try to get a room for the night in favor of the pup-tent he usually called home these days.

He usually had no mind for sleeping rough, but his bones ached and his heart was troubled. He could not put a finger on what made him jaw so much to Moon, even now. He had not talked to many, and never as much. He did not think it would help him, necessarily, but he never expected it would hurt him like this either. He could not shake the ghosts. Whiskey and a cotton–bed surely would go the right way, though.

XI

Giles left the barber shop with a jaunt in his step, pleased as pie at how things were looking. That mean old bastard barber shut the door sharply, really just some thing wood on a rickety frame on a platform, and locked the door behind him, but Giles scarcely noticed. It took a few seconds for him to feel the cold and it soured his mood. He wrapped his coat tighter around himself and started walking down the uneven porches of the shops, heading south down Hell

Street, where the bulk of the saloons were.

The storm was hot on his heels, and he wanted to be settled before anybody took his idea for their own.

XII

"What the hell is that?" Moon asked. He had slowed his horse and was looking to the south, to the horribly mismatched facades and porch roofs of the shotgun buildings and tents that lined the street as it neared the rail. Night had come but the clouds made even passive light impossible, only the swaying yellow of lantern light that managed to hit on something solid.

"What?" Josiah asked passively. He was tired and becoming agitated, a symptom of his advancing age that he hated more than the aches and pains. He had never been what could be called kind, but a gain in patience seemed to involve a gain in annoyance he did not much care for.

"There," Moon said, pointing slowly to the roof of a particularly large porch that made up the general store of the camp. Josiah and Moon slowed their horses and Josiah followed his gaze. There was a mass, something low and barely noticeable, a gray shape on the black of night. Without Moon's help, it's likely Josiah would never have seen it.

He gave a start as he noticed the shape was moving,

Josiah would call it prowling, an effortless slink across the rooftops. A man was walking with a purpose on the porches under the shape and they were going to be on top of each other in just a few seconds.

XIII

Giles heard it. He was not sure what it was, reminded him of the sound of a whip throwing luggage on a carriage. The boards on the porch above him creaked and he heard something moving, but it did not sound like footsteps, more like a sliding. Some damn fool drunk was up there, it seemed like, though that seemed damned foolish to Giles, this porch was about the most unstable thing he could imagine.

He stopped moving, looking up to the sound. He did not think any of these cowboys would get up on the roof of one of this places, but enough whiskey will do damn near anything to those animals.

Giles leaned against the flimsy railing of the porch he was under, one hand holding his coat closed, craning his neck to see what was on the roof of that porch, and to give him a taste of his mind for being a son of a bitch.

XIV

Both men looked but neither could understand what they saw. The shape was a little more sure now, thin and stretched, low and flat like an animal, slinking to the edge of the porch roof, right over where that man was standing still. It moved like a cougar, but it clearly was not a cougar. Josiah could swear it was almost a man, but he knew that was not right either, men do not move like that.

Moon slid off of his horse, bringing his rifle to bear, but stopped short of aiming. He found it hard to aim at something he could not understand, and he could barely see, it was little more than a brighter shadow among shadows. The angle was wrong and the light awful. He might only spook it if he missed.

"Hey!" Josiah shouted toward the porch, climbing off of his horse. The man across the street, leaning over the railing, looked up in surprise and alarm, nearly falling over as his hand lost its grip on the rough wood.

Josiah watched as the shape rapidly sprang into fast movement, clambering noisily over the edge of the porch roof, scuttling like a crab would. When it reached the edge of the porch, it extended what could only be called an arm, but it was nothing like Josiah had ever seen.

The arm was thinly muscular, long and wry, nearly six feet long, as far as he could tell, longer than any arm ought be. The hand at the end was equally large, with severely articulated fingers that ended in claws. Josiah could just barely make it out, like a big spider at the end of a tree branch. These clawed fingers got a grip on Giles' head, just under his jaw. He let out a loud shriek as he was lifted effortlessly into the air, clean off his feet like he were no more than a child.

Moon had moved closer and could now make the full shape, even if he did not understand what he was seeing. It was still lying flat, and the angle of the porch still made it hard to get a full assessment. He shouldered his rifle and with a hasty aim, he fired a shot.

Josiah was was following up close behind, his breath ragged and loud, either from exertion or fear, though Moon doubted it was fear. Josiah had drawn his pistol and was firing as well, careful, one at a time. Both men got off three shots before Giles was hefted too high into the air, blocking any further shots.

The creature, that thing, whatever it was, had pulled Giles up into a sitting position onto the roof. Giles continued to fight, swinging feebly against the thing, his screams growing more feeble but his actions growing more wild, desperate, like a loose crank. The creature's grip shifted and violently titled Gile's head to the side. It's head was like a man, mostly, but not like any man known to the people of that town. Moon and Josiah were close enough now, they could see it much more clearly. The creature had large, needle-like teeth that did not fit in the mouth. Josiah raised and aimed again, but before he could fire, the thing bit viciously into poor Gile's neck.

Giles let out a final, piercing scream as blood sprouted from his throat, pooling below him and dropping to the dusty ground in front of the porch, steaming in the cold. "Hell fire!" Josiah shouted, steadying his pistol and firing again. He could not tell exactly what he hit, but he heard the creature shriek in surprise and pain, dropping Giles and clambering back. Gile's body flopped uselessly and fell off the roof with a sickening sound.

The facade porch of the general store was not held down well and the creature moving erratically caused the thing to shake and creak loudly, shifting dangerously side to side.

Moon, his aim true and fixed, fired his last shot as the creature skittered back to the roof edge of the facade, and he saw it stumble as it cleared the edge and his sight. He heard it scramble loudly against the thick canvas of the tent. By now, several men had come out of the nearby saloon, just across the street, some with weapons drawn. Moon was hastily reloading as Josiah turned to the armed men.

"The roof! It went over the roof!" Josiah shouted, running as fast as he could past the dripping blood, to the side of the tent. There was not much clearance, the gaps between tents were just under two feet across at the widest part, and the large man struggled to fit. Behind him, he heard several men following and Moon shouting instructions to follow. There was another wild shot, some cowboy joining the excitement.

At the back of the general store, rows of dark tents in front of large fires, all mismatched and randomly pitched. Josiah could not see anything. He gripped his pistol tightly, trying to control his breath, keep his focus, force down the pain in his chest. He had two shots, and he dare not take the time to stop and reload the Dragoon.

It had been too long since he found something so formidable and the hardened veteran found himself afraid for the first time in years. In only a few minutes, he had found himself facing something unknown, something he had only imagined as a boy in the pews of his church. It felt wrong, like it belonged to a different time, place.

Three men now joined him close behind, none of which he knew, at least one sober, all with weapons drawn. All four men waited patiently, trying to listen over the shouts and confusion just a few feet away from them.

"There!" one of the men shouted, firing a shot blindly toward a bunch of tents to the west. Josiah would curse him for a fool if he had not seen the creature move, trying desperately to move from cover to cover. Josiah fired as well, and his shot missed, followed by more useless shots from those that joined him. One shot left. One of these fools was going to hit a man in these tents.

All four men took chase through the scrub-grass, darting around the corner pikes of the tents, but the creature outpaced them, now several rows ahead of them, moving almost silently, only the pounding of its feet on hard powder and the occasional glimmer of pale skin in the passing fire-light to betray it.

Josiah was out front, determined. He felt his chest tighten and his eyes swam, but he would not be defeated nor deterred, whatever this thing was, it was a threat, likely whatever had been hunting them, and they were all in danger. The other men following were keeping up, though the drunks were beginning to falter. One fired, a wild and poor shot, a chasing ring in their ears followed. The damn fool.

They were quickly coming to the end of the rows, having passed the main cluster of tents, thinning out before they reached the canyon's edge. As they got nearer to the arroyo, the sharper of them grew more concerned, as it was near impossible to see in the dark. Going over was a certainty of death in this darkness. There was a large gap in the tents, large enough for a coach, and the men took their cues from Josiah, cutting through the tents into the open prairie, running alongside the dark train tracks.

They were joined by another small gang, lead by Moon, quickly followed by Barnett and a small posse of gunfighters and onlookers, many of them wielding lanterns that helped the pursuers keep their footing. The creature was now in the clear, scampering low and fast, maybe twenty five feet in the lead, running in line with the tracks as well.

For the second time, Moon was reminded of a spider, a scuttling and loping thing, like a man on all fours, but faster than even a coyote. It sickened him to see it move. It did not fit, it was not a natural thing.

Moon took a large step to the left, away from the pursuing crowd and took a firm, sudden stand. He quickly shouldered his rifle and breathed out. The crowd slid past him, but he kept his aim firm and fired. A flash and burst, and the creature rolled awkwardly as it landed, letting out a mewling shriek that turned Josiah's stomach.

The creature's usual scrambling movement in the open recovered quickly and turned to a sort of gallop and it quickly put distance, until it slipped below the rim of the canyon and out of sight. It took almost a minute for the posse, nearly two dozen men, to reach the rim, careful to avoid the edge. A couple of the men immediately fired into the canyon, but surely nothing came of it.

The smoke hung in the still, cold air, and the shots rang through the canyon. Nobody at the rim moved, but the group was growing. The town had never heard as many shots at once and not even the cold could keep back the curious.

Josiah stepped a little further back, reloading his pistol carefully as Moon moved closer. "I hit it, I know I did," Moon said, panting, both from fatigue and no small amount of fear. "Whatever the hell it was, I shot it. How could it move like that after being shot?"

"I hit it, too," Josiah replied, panting great heaps of steam. "I heard them hit. I ain't never seen nothing like that."

Barnett approached both men, a look of cross concern across his already stern face. He had nothing to say to the men, just a look of bewilderment, his eyes wild. Josiah could only shake his head; his lungs burned, his chest ached, and he sounded bronchial, like some lunger. A drunk cowboy fired a random shot, startling those around.

"That's enough!" Barnett shouted. Harris now moved to the front of the group, his own Colt in his hand, the hammer cocked.

"Get these men back and inside, ask them what you can, I want them settled," Harris spoke quietly and with a finality that left no room for questions.

"Alright, let's back now, step back! Let's get inside!" Barnett shouted, holding up his rifle as a rally. Most were all eager to obey. Those that had seen something were a mix of frightened and confused, and those simply curious had nothing further to be curious about, and anybody remaining was simply tired of the cold.

As the crowd left quickly, Josiah and Moon brought up the rear, with Moon sidestepping, keeping an eye, and his rifle, on the blackness of the canyon. The night had become more quiet than was usual for Hell Street and it left a somber fear, carried on the bitter cold of a rising wind from the east.

XV

A small crowd had formed in front of the porch where Giles' body now lay, still lightly steaming but cooling quick. Most of the those not directly involved had moved back in from the cold, but the truly curious remained.

Josiah was none too eager to further bother with the matter, but with Moon moving off to see, he decided it best to follow. Having disbursed the majority of the tourists, Barnett pushed past and joined a crouched Harris, who was looking at Giles' remains with curiosity and concern.

"Tell me," Harris said patiently. Josiah noted that the lieutenant's gun was still in his hand. A cautious man. "Hell if I know," Moon said plainly. He would not take his eyes from the blackness of the country to the west and spoke over his shoulder.

"Was it an animal?" The wind kicked up and Josiah could smell the blood and the rot of empty bowels, the smell of death. He did not care to look at the mutilated body of the traveler. From the black sky, seemingly from the void itself, thicker snow flakes began falling, driven harder by the wind. The storm had a sense of the dramatic and was bearing down now.

Harris turned in his spot to look at Josiah, a look of open communication. Harris' breath was choppy and visible as thick steam, and his stubbled face seemed to be freezing as they spoke. Josiah could only shake his head. "I wish I could say. Weren't no man, but sure as hell wasn't no animal. It moved too... strange. Nothing I ever seen or even heard of. We hit it, at least twice, the boy and me. Didn't seem to care. Lost it down there in the canyon."

"Can we go after it?" Harris asked.

Moon spoke up first. "That'd be a bad idea." He noted the cross look of Harris and his voice caught, thinking he may have spoke too flippantly at a man like the lieutenant. He cleared his throat and spoke careful, like a scolded school-boy. "This thing, whatever it is... it's a hunter. It tore that feller up somethin' fierce, like nothing. Even a cougar don't do that, they sure as hell can't climb a goddamn building like this thing. We go down there, we don't come back, not in the dark. And not with this storm coming in."

Harris nodded grimly, only now holstering his Colt.

"We don't have to wonder what it is," Josiah whispered, his chest hurt from breathing in the cold air, but it was loosening now. He felt near ready to pass out. He crossed his arms tightly and wished for another coat.

"Why not?" Harris asked indignantly. He hated this, whatever it was, something that could not be understood or confronted. He was a man of certainty and action, and this night's violence defied both of those principles.

"It's death," Josiah answered simply. He wrapped his coat closer around him, feeling the bitter cold biting into his bones. He suddenly felt tired, useless, and exposed. "It's a thing, something we can't kill easily, and it means us harm and death. It'll likely keep doing just that, if we let it."

All three men turned suddenly at the sound of approaching footsteps. Abigail was approaching, cradling a double-barrel shotgun. Moon quickly turned back toward the direction of the rail, not wanting their backs exposed, as Harris and Josiah waited for Abigail to approach.

"What the hell is all this?" Abigail demanded.

"We don't rightly know," Josiah answered. "We saw... whatever it is we been worried about."

Abigail scoffed. "You get it?"

"No," Harris said. "Hit it, but it escaped."

Abigail scowled and looked to the fallen body, now barely recognizable as a man, covered in black-looking blood and mud. "Dear lord, that's a hell of a thing."

Moon nodded, still facing away from them, on look. "Reminds me of a wolf. Went for the neck. He bled fast."

Josiah grunted in effort, dropping to a knee, feeling

the strain climb his back. He would have pain tomorrow. He turned the body and Gile's head fell to the side sickly, his eyes wide and locked forever in surprise and fear. "It didn't take any bites out of him, just got him bleeding."

Harris leaned in, getting a closer look, his eyes looked into a hard scowl, bracing against the bitter wind. "So, it either couldn't get to that point, or it wasn't trying to."

"I don't think any animal would risk killing just to kill. Animals don't do that," Moon offered, his voice losing edge on the wind.

"Which means it just wanted the blood," Harris finished.

Abigail gave a cough of disgust. "So, it did all of it just to... suck on us?"

Josiah and Harris both turned to the young woman, with quite undetermined looks. There was a pause.

"Well, don't say it like that," Josiah finally answered.

"That's unlucky," Abigail answered, gripping her shotgun tighter. "At least we don't have to worry as much as we might." Neither Josiah nor Harris could guess what she meant by that. When they did not answer, Abigail could only cruelly laugh. "Both of you have walked that line, haven't ya? That death line? You both go to that dark place. You've brought death, and you have escaped it. You two are the best chance we have. If you two can work together, with help from these other boys, we may just survive this."

Abigail left the men speechless, back to the warmth and safety of her saloon, cradling her shotgun with conviction. Josiah and Harris could only stare at one another.

"Barnett," Harris finally said, rising and turning to the Pinkerton. "Get some men, have this cleaned up, we don't want panic. Double the sentries, pull them from the security or line workers, wherever you can, pay what needs paid. Make sure we watch the canyon edge."

Josiah chuffed and guided Moon toward the saloon and warmth. This snow storm was going to be a killer. The young hunter never looked away from the rail line, invisible in the darkness.

Barnett watched the two men depart before he answered. "We will, lieutenant. I'll post Ahlborn outside your office."

Harris shook his head, leading Barnett back toward the office, both bracing themselves in the incoming wind. The lieutenant frowned as he noticed the first of the snow flurries. "No, I think not. Have Ahlborn see the men outfitted, put him in charge of the defense. I want you to watch the town, some of these bandits may take advantage." He stretched broadly, and he seemed to be deep in thought. "Nothing gets in the way of the bridge."

They entered the railroad office and Barnett hastily shut the door. Harris immediately started feeding his stove, shivering. "Anything else?" Barnett asked.

Harris considered a moment, sitting next to his stove, wrapped in his coat. His mind raced to a thousand places, none of them places he wanted to go. His railroad project was becoming something else entirely and nothing in his experienced prepared him for something like this. Despite it, he was not a man to give up and would not start here.

"I don't think it wise to approach and ask, but if he has something to share, I ask that you tell me." Neither man needed to clarify who he was. "He may actually help, in some way."

"Can we trust him?" Barnett asked. His neatly trimmed mustache bristled as he frowned.

"He is as dangerous man as ever there was, if I guess right. He is a threat to anything he considers an enemy, that's clear." Harris stuck in another bundle of wood to his stove and rubbed his arms. "We can be thankful we are not his enemy."

THE ARIZONA TERRITORY

JANUARY 8, 1882

The storm brought troubles not seen in any recent memory. Sharp, biting wind brought sheets of frozen snow and rain seemingly without end, keeping all but the bravest battered within whatever shelter they could manage. By the second day, Harris was forced to pull his armed guards, as they risked frostbite and death in the storm. In the past couple days, five men had died in from the cold, mostly from the camps, and reports of disease was spreading.

As Harris grimly stared at the flat white of Hell Street, stuck uselessly in his office, his mind raced. On top of the men killed by the weather, six more men had died, though they only found four of their remains, all torn to pieces. Barnett had employed a couple hands for cleanup work of these remains, quickly stopping onlookers. Near as Ahlborn could tell, when he reported, there was not much concern within the camp yet, as people were too bundled up to gossip.

He would have gone completely mad if it were not that his office remained suitably warm, enabling him to continue to work as best as he could. A runner was expected soon, bringing word from the work camps beyond the canyon, stuck in the snow. He was still waiting, hoping something would come, that something would happen. All he could do was continue preparing. The expected bridge was going to be coming soon, and the time was not going to wait for weather or the violence they found themselves in.

Harris heard voices and rustling from outside, prompting him to grab his coat. The storm, while a vicious and fast thing, had disappeared as fast as it had come, leaving a quiet and somber weather in its stead. While still cold, the wind had died out and made being outside bearable.

The makeshift porch of the railroad office served adequate protection as Harris saw a rider come up Hell Street with difficulty, pushing his horse. The great beast moved up to the porch, allowing the rider to pass off a folded letter from his sack.

"Progress continues. Slow clearing as we go. 18 miles to go."

Despite the issues happening at camp, Harris would still see the project done, at all costs. Beyond the canyon, the rail gang had to proceed for the bridge to hook up to, on their mission west. This was better news then Harris had cause to trust.

"Thank you," he told the rider, a man he did not know.

"Yes, sir," the rider answered, keeping his horse moving in tight circles, clearing the snow around its legs. "Camp is pretty far off, with the snow its quite a journey now. Near a day"

"Any words of other problems?"

The rider pat his horse, who was protesting, likely due to the cold and circumstances. "A deserter, I think. One died in the cold, that I know of. That's about it. Foreman just gabbin', I don't reckon he was bothered by nothing."

Harris nodded and handed the rider a fifty cent piece and he left quickly. There was a livery of sorts set up on the other side of the rail line, just to the south of camp, set off from the edge of the arroyo. He watched the messenger ride off that way, indulging in fantasy, thinking of that man stabling his horse, and if he was a decent sort, maybe he would pat the horse and give it a treat. The rider would likely slip into one of the saloons, or the gambling halls if was a sporting man, anything to stay warm.

He was not sure why he spent any time thinking of

this rider. The center was holding, but as days wound on, the bridge was gathering ever closer, and his worry grew. The idea of failure had never really occurred to Harris, not now, or ever really. New Mexico had been effortless and now he worried.

He always saw it through, whatever that was, pushing through the impossible on sheer will. Indomitable. He had stopped the Indian raids attacking the railroad in Kansas, helped bust the union strike outside Tulsa, and along the way supervised untold miles of fresh iron track. Almost a decade of success and accomplishment. So, why now the doubt?

The animal attack, if it could be called that, gave him mixed feelings. Losing a half dozen men to such a creature certainly was not good in any context, but he had already lost more to disease and cold to this point. Death happened, especially on rail lines, and he had more than enough men to finish their task here. Once the snow cleared, he would be able to send riders off to Flagstaff and get a replenishment. Until such time, there was worry.

Harris was a practical man. He believed in the good book and God on high, but he found church distasteful, all the hand wringing and praise. He never thought God minded any of it, and he carried on his faith in his own way. He had never done or thought anything he found to be a frivolity or beyond what was before him. These attacks were shaking that standard.

He had not seen as much of the thing as Josiah or some of the others had, but he had seen enough, enough to know this was not an ambitious wolf or desperate cougar. This was something else, something new. While he was sure the desert held secrets from the likes of men, he doubted whatever this thing was came naturally. It did not feel right. He had never considered evil, the Real Evil like in the good book, but now he found himself thinking on it. Evil could be fought, and killed, but in the meantime, he, and his mission, would survive it.

It was several minutes of these thoughts before Harris realized he was cold. He had been ambling along the street, without any real direction, heading north. He must have a leak in his boot somewhere, he felt the wet and cold hit his feet. Cold and wet feet were a dangerous thing and he was not going to be laid up by it. Damn the bad luck.

He had turned back toward his office when Ahlborn came running up. Harris had seen little of him since reporting deaths during the storm, and he was surprised to see him now. "Lieutenant, I have been looking for you," Ahlborn said, short of breath. Harris noticed the Pinkerton was clutching his side in a stitch. "I heard something, I think you should see."

Without a word, Harris turned to follow Ahlborn, who waited patiently. The usual crisp uniform he wore,

Harris noted, had been replaced with simpler clothing, more closely resembling the sort worn by the locals. Ahlborn had always been able to blend in, which suited his work.

"What sort of thing is it?" Harris asked as he stepped up to Ahlborn. "Another body?"

"No, actually, a survivor," Ahlborn said, a tone of surprise. "I was in the hospital, which is just over here behind this row," he indicated vaguely in the direction they walked, "and there was a man there. Apparently he had shown up just before the snow storm. He is finally awake. I just think you should hear him out."

Harris nodded and double marched.

II

The hospital tent was set up much like those seen during the war. A low and wide layout, there were several rows of cots neatly arranged, and thankfully, most were empty. Injuries were not uncommon when working on a railroad, but the temporary work-stop had resulted in much fewer. One man lay off in the corner, in the final bouts of consumption, another was being treated off to the side, his thumb black from frostbite; he would lose it by the end of the week.

One of the beds in the center, closest to the wood stove that heated the tent, held a recovering Francisco de

Soto. He was exhausted and held several small cuts and bruises across his face, along with a fading sunburn that had been made worse by the cold, dry wind. Only the color in his face showed him to be alive.

Francisco was not asleep, but he had been keeping his eyes closed even when awake, when he could help it. He did not trust these men helping him, as he had never seen a place like this. They were clearly some kind of railroad operation, and he knew that could be bad for him, he had heard the railroad were unkind to foreign men like Francisco.

He heard steps coming toward him but he did not open his eyes until he heard them stop next to him. He opened his eyes quickly, suspiciously. Harris had taken a seat on the cot next to him, his coat wrapped rightly around him, his hands within his pockets. His wide gray hat had been pushed back. Despite his lack of knowledge, Francisco knew him to be a man of some importance, maybe in charge. The other man he had spoken to was standing behind this new man, quiet and watching. Nobody had really spoken to him before today.

"Are you alright?" Harris asked, his tone cordial. Ahlborn had been brief on details, and Harris was not sure to make of this man, except he clearly was no thief or gunfighter, just some poor soul that gotten lost in the desert, by the look of him. For his part, Ahlborn was present, but kept quiet, allowing Harris to take the talk where he wanted. Francisco sat up, with only minor difficulty. He was not terribly injured, but he had fallen from his horse a little less than a mile from the camp and it had broken a couple ribs. Breathing was getting easier but moving was a challenge. Harris waited patiently for him to sit up. Francisco panted for a moment, waiting for his breathing to settle before he tried to answer.

"I am okay. Tell me I broke ribs." Francisco did his best to keep his English clear, but could do nothing for his accent.

"That's good. Broken ribs are the devil, but a couple weeks you will be okay again." Harris cleared his throat and thought about his next step. This boy was clearly scared, Harris just was not certain by what yet. "My name is Lieutenant Jonathon Harris. What's your name?"

"Francisco de Soto. *De Espana.*"

Harris smiled at the young man. "What were you doing that you got hurt?" He tried to not make it sound like a challenge.

"I ride all night, got lost in the desert. Slept for a day. I saw town, horse trip, and I fell. I walked to town. Brought here." This statement took him a long moment to get out and Harris allowed him to talk, even reaching a hand to help stabilize Francisco when he started to lean. Both men were beginning to realize neither meant the other any harm.

"Riding at night is dangerous," Harris offered.

"Must. Had to run." Francisco's voice had gone quieter and Harris strained now to hear him.

"Run from what? Wolves? Bandits?"

Francisco shook his head and winced, the movement catching his side. Harris stood and helped Francisco lie back down, causing him to let out a few groans of pain as he readjusted. "Just lie here, it'll be easier to talk." After a moment, Francisco was breathing normally again.

"We were attacked. Not men. No wolves."

Harris: "Who is we?"

"*Hermano.* Hugo. On the trail."

"Making your way through?" Harris asked. The establishing questions were making him impatient, but he knew the man would get there.

Francisco just frowned in confusion, not understanding the question.

"Tell me about the attack," Harris offered. He leaned forward now.

"On trail, at first dark. We heard noises, I thought was wolf..." He trailed off, and his eyes glassed over. Harris had seen this, and knew this man had been brought back to whatever event happened. "It attack. *Rapido.* Fast. It got Hugo. I tried to fight..." His voice was broken, quivering. "*Esca cosa se lo llevo.* Dragged away Hugo. I run." Francisco was taken by heavy, wracking sobs, causing him pain that curled him.

Harris turned to look to Ahlborn, who looked concerned. Both knew the implication of this story; whatever this thing was, it moved far and fast. There were likely other victims, and it was not stopping. With a nod, Ahlborn was dismissed.

It took several moments for Francisco to get hold of himself. Harris placed a firm hand on his shoulder, the best he could do for reassurance. This was the closest he had seen to his time in the army, the senseless feeling of losing your brother to an enemy, something bigger than you can understand.

"*Lo deje morir*," Francisco repeated, his neck straining to keep his body still. His face was a deep red, twisted in agony of every kind.

"No," Harris answered. He knew some Spanish from his time along the border. He knew blame when he heard it. "No, you didn't. What attacked you? Did you see it?"

"*Si*. Yes. I saw. Dark, like a man, but not like man. Walk like dog, faster. Long arms."

Certainly the same thing, Harris decided. Whatever was killing his men got this man's brother. Harris patted his shoulder again. "You lie here, you are safe. We're going to get this thing, Francisco." Francisco could only nod, his eyes already a hundred miles away, his mind in a prison of memory. Harris hoped it would pass.

As Harris made his way out of the tent, the last he heard was Francisco praying.

III

Outside the hospital, Harris took a deep breath, bracing against the cold. Across the street, Ahlborn was speaking with one of the armed railroad men that he had tasked with patrolling, likely getting an update on the state of the camp to relay what they had learned from Francisco. Beside him, Barnett was listening intently, cradling his rifle tightly.

Ahlborn saw Harris waiting and finished up his conversation, running back across the street, Barnett in tow. Harris started to move with a purpose back toward the direction of his office, indicating to the men to follow.

To Ahlborn, he said: "I want you to get some men, about a dozen or so. Find the best. You'll need a tracker, or two. If you need to get some of the stringers in town, offer bounties. Whatever you need. I want you to find this thing." Harris kept a serious and stern tone and Ahlborn listened intently. Unlike Barnett, Ahlborn struggled without a direction, and was better used when he could be directed at a problem directly.

Barnett grunted. "We're going hunting? For this thing?"

Harris became impatient. "This... thing, it's killed nearly ten men we know, including that poor Spaniard's brother. There's likely more. We stay here, doing nothing, it'll keep picking people off. Word will eventually get around, once the snow clears, and we could be facing a revolt. The workers desert, or hell, they hang us. And the camp dies. The camp dies, the bridge doesn't get built, and the railroad dismisses us all. Because we failed." The idea of failure stung more to the men than the notion of death. Barnett would only nod.

Ahlborn understood and immediately starting thinking about how best to proceed. "There's a couple men I can call on here in camp, they should be able to help me find the rest."

"Good. Waste no time. Once you get everything you need, you ride out. Bring enough supplies for several days." They had made their way back to the office, and Ahlborn followed to the doorway. Harris unlocked a hard-box under his desk, handing over a stack of bills. "Anything you need. Get this thing, Ahlborn. Whatever it is, it's flesh and blood. You kill it and bring it back here."

Ahlborn gave a nod and he was off. Barnett had said nothing to this point and watched Ahlborn depart, turning his attention to Harris wordlessly.

"For you, get another man, and a spare horse. Buy it from the livery, if you must. I want you both to ride for the office in Flagstaff, and you bring back some fighting men. As many rifles as the offices has. Get bounty hunters, lawmen, even the outlaws. Anybody who can shoot straight."

Barnett said nothing, his already intense stare tightening. "What about your hunting party?"

Harris frowned, his brow furrowed. "They may not find it. It might win. I don't have answers here. I would rather double our chances."

Barnett found the sense in this. "What about you?"

"I will do what I can here, and continue to defend as best as we may. We still have some weeks until the bridge arrives."

From the hard–box, Harris handed Barnett his own stack of cash. Without another word, Barnett was off.

As his man left, Harris felt a mix of relief and apprehension. He had absolute faith in Ahlborn and Barnett and their abilities. There were no more dangerous men walking the earth, but this adversary was unlike anything else they, or surely anybody, had encountered. It killed at its leisure, seemingly without pattern.

Nothing they did was helping, and Harris would not be put on the defensive.

IV

Josiah was listless.

The storm had battered him, and the cold was becoming something he struggled with constantly. He feared he would soon have to move on, probably more south toward the border where it stayed warmer.

Like many of those that paid attention, he was well aware of those that had died in the past couple nights. He had not slept well, always wanting to remain aware, and this dulled his already distracted senses. He hated that feeling.

Walking through the snow, while not terribly deep and already beginning to melt, was difficult for him. His knees ached and his back was too sore to straighten to full height without a sharp pain that ran down his leg. As much as it pained him, the movement helped keep him more loose and diminished his aching pain.

His walk took him past the center of town, remarkably quiet for the time of day, most staying in whichever shelter they could manage. On his way, he had noticed that many of the poorer of the camps with lean–to tents had seemed to find other arrangements, as they could not be found now, either in or out of their camps.

As he passed some of the only structures that existed in town, he took note of the railroad office, which had Harris and one of his men at the door. He watched the guard, a man whose name he had never bothered to learn, take off quickly down the road toward the livery.

Harris stood in the doorway, looking off after his

man. While Harris was not too much younger than Josiah, by his estimation, he had seemed more youthful in his bearing. No longer. The officer looked weary, beaten, and older than his years. He appeared to not have shaved since arriving, his face looking rough and slack. Josiah doubted he was sleeping any better than he.

Both men saw the look of the other and neither knew quite how to proceed. There had been no animosity from either man, quite the opposite in fact, but both were still apprehensive. When Harris leaned wearily against the side of his doorway, a look of surrender, Josiah altered his path and approached.

"You look dead on your feet," Josiah offered, standing a few feet from the doorway. He took a moment to appreciate the sun on his back.

"Kind of you," Harris replied. He did not smile, but it felt good to have a man such as Josiah there to remind Harris he was still just a man. Both men were quiet a moment, unsure of what to say. "I had a question for you."

Josiah's mouth went around for a moment, his eyes narrowing. "What sort?"

"I know you have little reason to care. About this town, these people. You could have just gone and left them to all of it. Probably should have. But you stayed. You've helped." Harris paused a moment, Josiah just staring at him passively, a stalwart immovable object. "You have offered me insight, and you haven't fought with me, as I expected you might've. My question is why."

Josiah was amused, shuffling his feet as he considered his answer. "I have thought about that. You have vision. You and the men like you will forever be pushing for more, for bigger." He gestured to the rail to emphasize his point. "You cannot be stopped. At least, the idea behind you can't be. I have no vision, no great purpose, no goals, I just want to be left 'lone. My dreams died long ago, whatever they may have been. That wasn't your doing." He paused a moment. He rarely talked so much, or in such a manner, especially to some Yankee officer. "We aren't enemies, lieutenant."

"I am pleased to hear it," Harris said. "I wouldn't want a man of your sort as my enemy." Harris took the opportunity to pry off his boot, frowning at the water falling out of it. He saw the damage to the seam where the boot met the sole; he would need new boots.

There was a call off to the distance and both turned to watch Ahlborn, now in heavier attire and on a saddle mare, riding deeper into the camp on his errand. "Your doing?"

"Hunting party," Harris replied. "Try to find… whatever it is. Ahlborn is getting a posse."

Josiah paused, doubting how he should best say it. "You should pull them boys back."

Harris stared in disbelief, sliding his damaged boot

back on; it was better than nothing at the moment. "Why? Ahlborn is a crack shot. If they can put it down, all the better."

"We're not the hunters here, lieutenant. This isn't war. This isn't a fight, it's a goddamn turkey shoot. We're the turkeys. Them boys would be better here. I can't promise we can kill this thing, but more guns gives us a better chance."

Harris sighed. The veteran was not wrong, on the surface. Even when he set off Ahlborn to the task, he doubted the success of such a mission. But surely he could not sit on his hands and do nothing, not while people died.

"Doing nothing is the same as giving up," Harris answered. "Ahlborn may not get it. But he might. All we can do is try. I am going to have night patrols, try to see if we can catch it. We know we can harm it, which means we can kill it."

Josiah was quiet a moment, turning to look to the camp behind him. "I hope you're right. I hope you succeed, for all our sake. As long as you don't give up, I suppose we all have a chance."

V

The weather, which had been unseasonably bitter in the buildup of the snow storm, was finally bearable again, with clear skies and a softer wind. Spending any length of time in the open air was still uncomfortable, but it was becoming right tolerable in comparison.

Enjoying some open air, Ahlborn felt good about their chances. True to his charge, he had enlisted the help of two of the railroad's finer security officers, Parker and Stewart. Neither looked the part, both being smaller men in stature, but they were steadfast and resolute. They had volunteered immediately.

Between the three of them, within fifteen minutes they had gathered a formidable party. Among them were several men from the railroad, most of them from security, but in particular was a stone mason named William that was strong as a bull and meaner than a snake. Two civilians had joined them, as well. A hunter–tracker, Decuir, had signed on with little persuading.

In total, they numbered ten, less than hoped for, perhaps, but a strong group. Decuir had led the way, following the path out of town to the north, taking his time to find a solid path used by their adversary. It had not been easy. Despite the reported size of the creature, that of a man at least, it did not leave a trace like any man typically did. Within an hour, he had found a trace, a minor disruption in melting snow.

Decuir, a French–man down from eastern Canada, had come from a family of traders since before the War of the Conquest. He was a tough man, clever and formidable.

He had known of the attacks in town and was eager to calm this matter. Decuir's coon skin hat was a source of some private amusement for Ahlborn that he shared with no-one. The night was getting on and following the trail was becoming more difficult. Decuir had dismounted, walking slowly, following the strange track. Ahlborn followed close behind, leading Decuir's mare.

Decuir spoke with an odd accent, quiet and measured. "Most animals, especially the predatory sort, they move carefully, conserving energy. The tracks of this... creature, whatever it may be, they're damn strange. It seems to move fast, its a loping gait, almost like a horse at gallop. But it moves at this... angle." A dense, muddy spot formed in clay-like soil had given him the best look at its tracks to this point. Decuir, puzzled by what he saw, motioned Ahlborn over, puzzled.

"What is it?" Ahlborn asked.

"Look at this." Decuir was kneeling, looking closely to the tracks in the drying mud. "This is it's marks, here and here." He indicated the front and back. "Three feet, little more. It moves fast. Doesn't move in a straight line, seems like its turned as it moves. I've never seen that." Decuir took a deep breath, shifting to the front track. "This doesn't look like a foot."

"What does it look like?" Ahlborn asked, curious. He had no real experience with such things, and had not spent much time in the frontier, save for the past couple of years. He was not as comfortable in the wild, but he adapted quickly, and wanted to learn.

Decuir seemed to struggle with the right words, starting and stopping many times. Finally, he balled his hand into a fist and stuck it into the track. Though it was a little bigger, it was clearly the exact same shape.

Ahlborn said nothing for a moment, before finally answering: "It's getting dark and cold. Let's set up camp."

VI

The atmosphere in town was lighter than it had been since before the storm.

Largely thanks to the change in the weather, more of the residents in Diablo were about in the town. The saloons and eating counters were packed full. The chuck wagon at Abigail's had salted pork, stew, and biscuits, doing good business.

At Abigail's. Josiah had found his usual spot at her bar, though he had decided to not drink. He had only willingly forgone available alcohol a few times in his life, but this seemed an appropriate time. While he had no reason to doubt Harris' assessment of his man, Ahlborn, Josiah was less than sure of this hunting party's chances for success. A clear head and steady hand seemed in order.

A whole team of people had chased and shot at this thing and had made no real progress toward harming it. It seemed likely to Josiah that tonight, like every other, would end with bloodshed, or a missing man, maybe more. Now that the weather had cleared, the snows were melting, and another night of violence would start an exodus. Panic would rise and the situation would worsen.

He considered that thought a moment. He had stayed through this out of a necessity, stuck as he was by the weather and the likelihood of not making it back to town. But now, he could leave at first light and if he rode hard, he could be in Flagstaff by sundown. From there, it would be a simple matter to keep heading west, see if he can find something worth finding, same as he had done until now.

He owed these people nothing, and there was little help he could really provide. Harris seemed to have brought him into his confidence, but the reasons for this still eluded Josiah. What help could he really provide a man like Harris? He was just an old man, broken, disillusioned.

"You look troubled," Abigail said. Her voice, softer and sweeter than he recalled it ever being, cut through his thoughts. She was standing just off, her head low, like her tone. She looked concerned.

He gave a brief, pained smile and shook his great grizzled head. "Lost in my thoughts," he answered, dismissive. He had never wanted to trouble Abigail, for tough thing that she was, Josiah knew there to be a part of her, some losing part, that clung to decency and tenderness. Fostering that would only lead to her calamity, and he would not be responsible for such a thing.

"Must be some tough thoughts," she replied, her eyes brows still pinched in worry.

"Might be true to say." He hoped this could be the end of it she could go back to her business. But after a moment, she still lingered, unchanged. "Something on your mind?"

"Yes," she said simply, her blunt tone cutting an edge to her words. "Something I have wondered since first I met you." She did not wait for leave before continuing. "Aside from that Lieutenant Harris these past couple of days, and that young man, you had no words to say to any man here. Aside me. There must be reason for that."

Of all the things he thought she may ask, that was not among them, and it caught him off his guard. He had hoped to never invite the confidences of these people, passing through as he was.

"It has been my custom," he answered. "I am passing through only, and I will be gone before long, and you will lose all memory of me. As it should be."

"That weren't an answer," she replied, swift and cruel.

He chuckled, amused. Her response only reinforced her point, though she would not know that. "You rightly guessed I fought in the war. Like most of us old enough did. I answered the call of the cause without question. For my country, for my brothers. There were many reasons. Some good, some bad. I fought to stop the change I saw ruining our way of life." He felt winded, like had had been running, despite having not moved. "We lost, and it all continued. Progress, they call it. That's fine. I can stay ahead of that." Abigail said nothing.

He paused a moment, almost at a pant, before he continued. "I had a young wife. She was a pretty thing. Don't know what she saw in me. I wasn't handsome, even then, but she loved me, and I her. A simple thing, that sort of love. Wasn't much to it, just... got to be. I left her there, for the war. She asked me not to, of course. Most wives did not wish it, you can imagine." He smiled here. "Before I left, she baked me a pie. Blueberry. Threatened to fatten me up too much to fight."

His voice become strained, and his tone shifted, his usually slow speech dragging even further. "She was so head-strong. A farmer's daughter, she knew how tough life was and she met it honestly." A longer pause here. The saloon around them continued its loud, jovial march but neither paid any attention. They might as well have been all alone in the whole world. "She died three months before the war ended. Heard she took ill, never did find out from what. Doesn't provide me any comfort to know, anyhow. She went fast, I was told."

"Good lord," Abigail whispered.

"It happened to many of us. I had no right to expect any different. I heard about it, in a letter. I never went home. What home was there? I dropped that letter in Tennessee and I have been keeping ahead of that... progress, as it's called, since then." He swallowed hard, his body felt like stone.

"I am sorry to hear that," Abigail said softly, though what might have been compassion or care was cut with a tone of bitterness. It would have sounded disingenuous coming from any other. "But why tell me that?"

He answered quickly and with no small amount of pain. "You remind me of her."

Abigail was taken aback by this. Since she was a little girl, life had been hard, and she had learned the ways of life and men in the harshest and most cruel of ways. She had been chased and desired by any number of men, and some had gotten close enough for consideration. But not one of them had something that personal to share with her, that meaningful.

She struggled to find something to say to him, but he saw this and waved his hand dismissively. "Don't let it weigh any on you," he said. She saw his eyes raw and felt a tenderness for the old soldier she had not before. She understood now, the sort of man who wanted nothing from her, because he had already found it. He saw value in her for the sake of being her.

"Does this mean you will be moving on now?" she asked, a tone of sass.

"We all will, before too long, I reckon. I told Harris I would stay until I saw this through. May be this will give me what I have been searching for."

"And what's that?" she asked.

He did not answer her.

VII

Ahlborn's camp was fully setup well before proper nightfall. The cold was settling back in a big way, the open desert losing any trapped heat it had gathered, and a large fire had been built to accommodate. The tents had been erected in a circle as close to the fire as was prudent. Some of them men were doubling up, leading to six tents. Decuir had a low tent, different than the rest, just big enough for himself to fit into. He sat in front of it now, warming up and drawing in his journal.

William, the able bodied stone worker, was just off in the dark, chopping more wood for their fire. Parker, out of an abundance of caution, had taken two of the others out to scout around. Nobody really thought that the creature would fall into their lap so easily, but caution was duly warranted. Whatever this thing was, it was clearly vicious and ravenous, a killer.

Secretly, Ahlborn was certain they were going to be little more than a baited trap, a tempting target. He hoped he was wrong, but as he saw it there were only two options. Clearly, this was a night hunter and while it was active in the hunt, they would be at a disadvantage. So, they either waited for it to come to them, a unified force, or they tracked it down to its den during the day, where it would be vulnerable.

Out of caution, while Parker patrolled, Stewart had taken up security around the camp. He and two others were stationed between the tents, their rifles at the ready, peering into the darkness. Behind them, the fire crackled pleasantly. Ahlborn walked restlessly around the fire, keeping each side of him warm. He doubted he could sleep in such a situation, but he would have to try at some point. He was uneasy, but they had a good chance for success. As he passed Decuir, drawing in detail, he paused a moment.

"So, what's your thought?" Ahlborn asked. Decuir did not show any sign he had heard the Pinkerton until he spoke without lifting his head.

"I wish I knew," Decuir said grimly. He set his charcoal pencil down and sighed. "This... thing. From what I have been told, and what I see from its tracks, I would say it's a man. A large, strange man, but a man."

"I don't think it's a man," Ahlborn said defensively.

Decuir shook his head. "Not like we know, but... something like it. I don't know. It's no cat, no bear or wolf, and there's nothing out here that's even close to this sort of thing. Look..." Once again, Ahlborn knelt next to Decuir, who had drawn a crude map onto the previous pages of his journal.

Decuir continued. "This thing, it's going in a big circle. You see that in ambush predators. Waiting for an opening. But it's not hunting like an animal, they don't attack just to do it. It's for food. Defense. This... is slaughter. It's moving in these big circles, like it's keeping things corralled. You see that in wolves. It's... damn strange."

Ahlborn frowned, unsettled. Hunting an animal, something instinctual and driven only by impulse, is much different than pursuing something that thought like a man.

"Where's Parker?"

VIII

Parker wanted to be back. He hated going out in the dark and the cold. It was completely unsafe, but he felt it a good idea, in case they had happened to make camp in a less than ideal spot. So far, his concerns seem to be for not. He had to admit his experience in defending work camps from bandits and saboteurs was entirely different than hunting down a dangerous animal.

The two men he had brought with were not the most experienced, but they were eager and both appeared to be fearless. Thankfully, as the clouds gave way, the moon was still mostly full and provided some decent light for them to see by.

"We should head back," one of the men said, a man named Eugene, approaching Parker on horseback, tentative. It did not seem to be fear that drove him, but a dreadful sort of caution.

Parker nodded, both men practically on top of each other now. "Agree. Where's Aaron?"

Eugene shook his head. "I haven't seen him, but he can't be far."

"Aaron!" Parker suddenly shouted, at about half volume. If they were not known, it would be best to not make it easier to find them. There was no answer beyond the wind, lightly moving through the scrub. Parker's horse suddenly shuffled, neighing in protest.

"Spooked," Eugene said quietly, his own horse now moving restlessly. "They smell something."

Parker sucked his teeth and tucked the butt of his rifle up on his hip, straining to see around him. The moon provided a pale, listless light on the desert, but details were washed out in shadows. Both men waited a moment, but nothing stirred save their horses.

"Think it got him?" Eugene asked, drawing his pistol.

"I don't know," Parker admitted. "Make your way down those rocks, the camp can't be more than a mile over that rise. Let's just move quickly."

Both pulled on their horses bridles, trying to guide them down into a flat part that would enable them to move around the large rock they were stuck behind. The horses were not cooperating fully, clearly scared and beginning to panic. They neighed in louder and longer bouts.

"Hell fire," Parker whispered. He gave his horse a kick, startling the beast, driving it forward. He bumped past Eugene and managed to get onto the path, with Eugene right behind him. He checked the ground before him and gave his horse another nudge, but it only reared back, crying out and spinning in a circle.

Eugene managed to avoid the panicked horse, tucking away to the right, but his horses leg caught a large stone, tripping the horse and spilling them both out. Eugene hit the ground hard, knocking the wind out of his lungs, leaving him gasping.

Parker heard Eugene fall, but it was taking all he had to keep his horse stable. He was not the greatest horseman and he was losing his grip on the situation. In desperation, he slid off his horse as fast as he could, falling to his knees painfully. His horse took off like a shot.

Gaining his footing, he turned to Eugene, writhing on the ground. His own horse was regaining its composure and trotting away. Eugene was still gasping helplessly and as Parker knelt beside him, it was already too late and Parker could only manage a single scream before he was grabbed.

He felt the claws penetrate his skin, through his throat. Searing pain wracked him, clouding his thoughts. He could see the fountains of blood pouring from him onto the dirt and he felt his body weaken. He had no fight left, and could only watch helplessly as he was tossed to the ground. Eugene was set upon before he could rise to his feet, screaming wildly. Parker's hand could not reach bleeding his neck before it all went black.

IX

Ahlborn heard it clearly.

Within seconds, each man in camp had risen to their feet and brought their rifles to bear. Stewart and his two guards stayed on the back end of the tent circle, their rifles at the ready, shouting to each other. So far, nobody could see anything.

It seemed Ahlborn's suspicion was right on. He and Decuir each picked up their repeaters, scanning the darkness around them. The fire, an unwisely large pyre, ruined their night vision, making the night just beyond their own camp that much darker.

William came to within the camp circle, cradling the ample wood ax he had been chopping with, seemingly electing for the weapon over a pistol.

"Get that fire out!" Ahlborn barked loudly, to nobody in particular, his voice filled with desperation. The fire may keep it away, but that is not a long solution and there was no guarantee it would work. They did not need to defend themselves, as much as they needed to kill it. Now was their chance.

Within seconds, William and Decuir began kicking piles of sand onto the fire, causing the great flames to falter and flicker, casting eerie shadows onto the tents around them. After a moment, William had grabbed and dumped his water onto the remaining fire, damping the last of the light and heat, filling the camp with thick white smoke.

Nothing and nobody moved. The only sound now was the crackling and sizzling of the embers and the heavy breathing of the men around the camp. As quietly as they could, they began to move into the middle, buried in smoke and dark.

Minutes passed before anyone spoke. "Anything?" Stewart called out, tension heavy on his tone of voice. The others could hear him shuffling in the dirt beyond the tents.

"Nothing!" a man answered back, nobody was quite sure who.

"Quiet!" Ahlborn caution, his rifle shaking. The cold was settling into his fingers and he struggled to keep his arms up. Beside him, on one knee, Decuir was quiet and scanning, his repeater resting against his leg.

On the west side of the camp, there was a hasty shout and the sound of a shot, the flash of it washing over the camp. All men turned their gaze that way and each yelled, a hurried, jumbled mess of frantic noise. Ahlborn quickly side-stepped the fire and moved toward the shot, his gun at the ready, his eyes watering in the smoke and cold air.

He and Stewart both reached it, flinching at the sight of each other. Below them, one of their men lie dead, his discharged rifle beside him. The moon gave just enough light for them to see the body splayed unnaturally, his torso clawed and torn, blood covering him.

"Where is it?" Stewart whispered, darting his eyes and rifle into the distance. Before Ahlborn could speak, there was another scream from the other side of the camp. Away from the scream, out of sight, another shot. Panic set in.

They turned and went back to the center of the camp. Decuir and William had remained, side by side, Decuir still in a kneel, his rifle up and held expertly. "Anything?!" Ahlborn shouted to them, all thought of quiet long since abandoned.

"I can't see anything!" Decuir yelled, his eyes in the direction of the last scream. The four men stood together, seeing nothing, hearing less. The shots slowly cleared their hearing, leaving a faint ring in each of them. Silence again.

"It's picking us off," Ahlborn said, tremendous effort given to keeping his voice low and steady. For the first time he could recall, he felt he had taken a grave misstep, and unless they were very lucky, they would all mortally pay for that mistake.

"There!" William shouted, startling the men. Through a break in the tents, the moon showed a flurry of dark gray, a shape moving like nothing from nature, a scampering movement. Ahlborn was sure he could hear a snarling whine, but he could not place the direction it came from. Then, another movement, the next tent, slower this time.

No details could be made, not in that light, but they could see the creature, a hunched, smoothly moving shape in the distance. Low and dark, they kept losing the edge, but the mass of disgusting color kept it visible, pale in the moonlight. Without a warning, William, his wood ax still in hand, pushed between the men and ran to the creature.

"No!" Decuir yelled, but it was little use. William made the distance in three bounds, ax raised high overhead. The creature waited patiently, not moving until William was within arms reach. With an unholy speed, before William could drop the ax, the creature darted forward, lengthening its body sickeningly and swiping with one of its long arms.

William, a large man of nearly three-hundred pounds, was lifted from his feet and tossed into the tent beside him, knocking the entire thing down onto him, snapping the support pole clean in two. Before he had landed, the creature leaped, frog-like, from its position onto him, its pointed elbows cocked off wildly to the side while it dug and tore at William. The ripping sounds could be heard over William's screams.

Decuir, Ahlborn, and Stewart all fired, littering the area with gun–smoke, lead, and light. A spectacle of light and sound and then silence again. There was no sign of the thing, and no noise, no movement from William; he was dead.

"Decuir," Ahlborn whispered, his hands white knuckled on his rifle. "Can you get to your horse?"

"For what?" he demanded, his own rifle sweeping the camp.

"You need to warn the town. They need reinforcements, help, something. We can stall it long enough for you to get away," Ahlborn said, his voice still even, though his mind raced and his heart felt near spent.

"You'll die!" Decuir protested, but Stewart had already moved, grabbing Decuir and pushing him back to where their horses were hitched.

"No time, go!" Stewart yelled, steeling himself. He brought himself up to his full size and clumsily slotted a round into the magazine of his repeater. "Get!"

Taking a cue from his ally, Ahlborn also drew up, feeding a round, two, into his rifle. They would only get one or two shots, should be enough. He could not see, but he was sure the creature was just over that tent wreckage, waiting.

"Now!" Ahlborn shouted, hearing Decuir scramble behind them as he and Stewart advanced, each taking turns firing into the direction they were sure the creature waited. Decuir mounted his horse and gave it a strong kick, sending the animal quickly down the pass they came in on.

As they saw Decuir ride off, both fired more, drawing attention. Too late, Ahlborn saw movement to his left, dropping his spent rifle he reached for his sidearm but he was too slow, getting only a single, but true, shot. With a high pitched whelp, the creature stumbled but still ran into him, knocking him off of his feet, running straight through and clambering onto Stewart.

Stewart fired from his hip, missing wide, as the creature's left hand, broad and spider-like, effortlessly gouged into the skin of his throat, destroying his neck and pulling out its innards, leaving him to futilely gasp and gurgle in a fountain of his own blood.

Ahlborn tried to recover, clambering to his feet, but

he only made it halfway. The creature rounded on him, spinning fluidly on its spot. Ahlborn felt his stomach open, like that poor son of a bitch on the edge of their camp. Already, the light was going around the edges of his vision. He could still see the thing. So close, now. If only he had another shot, but his fingers had stopped working.

Ahlborn's fading vision could make no details, and it continued to shrink in, his vision going black. He had remained standing, feebly holding onto his dropping guts. He no longer felt any heat, or any cold.

When the creature knocked him to his back and began to feed on him, he did not feel that either.

THE ARIZONA TERRITORY

JANUARY 9–10, 1882

The more agreeable weather was not meant to last. The skies remained clear but a brutal cold had settled into the mountain over the night. Hovering at zero, the unforgiving dry air stabbed with every breath. The normal nightly activity of town was diminished to only the most stalwart.

Just after midnight, the settled cold hit the camps harshly. An older worker known only as Tucker had been struggling with the cold, his health diminishing since their camp left Albuquerque. He had hoped to make it to somewhere warmer, but he never did, dying that very night. Two others would join him, including a youngster from Alabama that had lied about his age to work the railroad. Two young men, only a year in country from China, were shivering in their poor tent, with its many holes allowing every breeze and ounce of cold in. One of them would not live to see daybreak, either.

Out in the rolling foothills that made up the open prairie, far to the south–east of Cañon Diablo, a pair of wagons had hunkered down for the night, hoping to wait out the worst of the dark and cold, especially with the youngins they had with them. The youngest, a little girl that only came to the knee and could not yet talk, was bundled tightly in the best wagon, buried under a pile of recently bought furs. She had never slept as soundly. The wagoners were camped no more than four miles from Ahlborn's camp and would never learn how close they had come to death.

By two in the morning, though nobody had bothered to check the time, Barnett had been able to accomplish what he had set out to do, riding back with nearly thirty strong, beating the devil out of the horses to make it back as fast as they could. Nearly three thousand of the railroad's dollars had gotten the result he was after, a motley collection of railroad security officers, a bounty hunter, a handful of trappers, and a couple of likely outlaws that were ready to help for the cash and thrill. The cold hurt them and slowed them, but Barnett's steely demeanor kept up the pace. Not a word of complaint was heard the trip back.

All throughout the northern part of the territory, many fought hard for life and comfort, and most succeeded.

The tragedy of the lost was not lost on the survivors as the dark cold rolled on.

II

Despite the brutal cold, Brooks had to start his day early. He was never sure of the time, it mattered little to the foreman, he just knew it was dark and damn cold. He had adjusted to the cold and high altitude better than most of the others, having come down from the Dakotas originally, but even for him, this recent weather had been too much for him. Age, more than likely, played a roll. Despite some others, though, he had no illusions of quitting, and would likely die in his work tent. This suited him fine.

He slept in a bunk in a small tent just behind one of the larger mess tents. Most mornings, the smell of coffee, rancid though it may sometimes be, was a welcome way to wake, starting at sunup. Today, he had to be up before his usual custom. In the pitch black of his tent, he moved slowly, unburdening himself from several layers of blankets, including a bear pelt he had traded for that he was particularly fond of.

He dressed quickly, working against his protesting back and pained joints. The longer he spent dressing, the greater the chance the cold could settle in his bones and make it harder to get warm again. Spring could not come fast enough.

As troubling as the cold was, these continued attacks were of greater concern. The abandonment, and that fight yesterday, was one thing, but Harris had done a great job with stopping it. Brooks' greatest fear was in the event the attacks did not end, or escalated further, the workers could riot or perhaps even destroy it in their fear. If things became too difficult, the following businesses could leave as well, further damaging the men's resolve. Like Harris, Brooks had no intention of abandoning his duty.

He had faith in Harris. He knew anything and everything humanly possible would be done, and the situation would never be abandoned or left to chance. There are just limits to what a man can do, even one as determined as Harris.

There was little for Brooks to do about these concerns, but he felt it prudent to be prepared for them. He had become personally invested in the completion of this line, having worked it since it began. While he did not share the same zeal as Harris regarding its completion, he desired the same goal, for the same reasons.

Finally dressed tightly, he was already cold, feeling it settling into his toes, and it made him regret getting up early. If he was lucky, there would be coffee ready.

III

Thomas Moon had fared better than most in the wake of the storm. Certainly his youth had helped him, but beyond this he had seen the storm coming and his life on the back of a horse had taught him a few things. Before tucking into his tent, a rather spacious one just to the south of the camp where the creature had first attacked, he had gone to the trading post and traded for a couple of heavier furs, one of which he had draped over the top of his tent, allowing for better warmth, a trick he had picked up from a Crow some years prior when he was first starting out.

He spent the entirety of the storm bundled safely and comfortably, eating his stores of dried meat and a can of peaches that had half frozen. He spent most of the time sleeping, and thinking. He was not learned, having skipped out of most of his schooling, but he new animals and the hunt, and like many in town that knew better, he was troubled by this creature.

What sort of thing will not go down with several shots like that? By the time the first hints of dawn crept up that morning, he was all too ready to get out of his tent and stop thinking about it, and just get to hunting.

IV

The brutal cold slowed down the start of the day, but it could not stop it. As the first of the sunlight crested, the billowing smoke from the camps and stoves settled low throughout the town, glowing gold and bright. The smells mixed into something that could not be determined, but it did a good job of rustling all but the most stubborn from sleep.

Rookwell, the surly barber that had the custom of Giles Montgomery before he died, was one of the stubborn. Tucked into the back of his shop tent was a place for him, a suitable straw bunk next to a high quality stove that he kept heavily fed. He detested the cold and would do all he could to avoid it. He would open his shop when he felt like it and not before. In the meantime, he would sleep through the worst of the cold.

In her saloon, Abigail was up early, hastily giving instructions to her recently hired cook. At Abigail's request, in the back of the ample saloon tent, Amos had erected an impressive kitchen, with his ample cauldron at its center, his chuck wagon closely tucked up behind him. Since most went into Abigail's anyway, she had invited him into a permanent position in the back.

The cold did not bother Amos this morning, the heat from his cooking fire and nearby stove keeping him plenty comfortable, even in the cold. Drenched in a heavy coat, many sizes too large for him that he stole from a buffalo hunter some years prior, Amos busied himself with a large batch of bacon and beans. Abigail had expected a strong push for coffee and a warm breakfast from most of the town, and she planned to deliver.

V

Josiah had not slept.

Worry and discomfort had made it difficult to sleep, and by the early morning he had given up. About the time Brooks was making his way out, Josiah was bundled tightly and walking briskly up to Abigail's. He knew it was one of the places in town open and warm at all hours.

While he walked and waited, he could little else but think. When he first arrived, there were only two drunks at the bar, led by a man Josiah had no knowledge of. The drunks paid him no mind, and he returned the favor, setting himself at the end, which had become his standard place, it seemed.

It took no time for him to become irritated by the drunks. "You two!" he shouted brusquely, startling both. "Clear out of here with that!" They quickly departed without a word.

Despite being troubled, he liked the temporary quiet.

In the pre–dawn dark, a single idea predominated his attention. By all that he could see, and all he could imagine, it seemed likely he would not get out of this situation without bloodshed. Whether his own or that of this creature that haunted them, he could not be sure.

He did not mind the idea of dying. He could freely admit to himself he had been inviting it for many years now. He knew it was not possible to just give up living, that was the act of a coward, and he could not stomach that notion. But dying in this fight, that would satisfy him.

His time in the war was different than this. In those battles, he was fighting his countrymen, his brothers. It was always a fight of necessity, an opposition of ideas, and it would always going to send before the total destruction of either side. This was different. This was simply life and the loss of it, and this thing, whatever it may be, would continue to draw blood until they did the same.

By the time his thoughts abated him, he could feel and hear the bustle of the town beginning. The golden light of day hit the road, lighting the town, and starting another day.

VI

Harris had not slept either.

He kept his boots on, buried under his blankets and

a fur he bought from the general store, staring out into the dark, lost in his thoughts. For his comfort, he had stayed in his bed and felt the urge to get out of it about the time that his foreman did, but he lacked the same drive to leave the warmth of his bed. His back pained him horribly, his bed seemingly splitting sometime in the past two days, but still he remained. On his face, he could feeling the penetrating cold, hurting and irritating his dry skin. He was miserable. He knew the weather was not the only thing causing him distress, but it felt like a boon to blame the cold.

Despite it only being half a day since he sent Ahlborn, he already felt great concern. The nature of this thing they fought eluded all reason, and perhaps it had been a mistake to think some men could such a thing down, alone in the desert. There was still a chance they would succeed, and the project would be safe. He was not a praying man, but he spared every moment he could for his departed man.

He had long since noticed the sun through the meager window and breaks in the wood sides of his hovel. His day needed to start but some tremendous reckoning had settled in his chest. He could not be sure, but he reckoned the fantastic nature of what they faced had left him stymied. All obstacles before him in the past could be handled with ease, even if it was violence.

While he tried to contemplate what means of force was still available to him, he heard a loud commotion from outside and decided he had better get up.

VII

The sunlight, and what little warm comfort it could manage, had the main stretch that ran alongside the track lit up, attracting some from the safety of their beds. The day, while already getting on, seemed to be leaving most behind, especially those that could find some semblance of rest. Movement was slow, though some were indeed attracted to the swelling smoke from Amos' cooking fire at the saloon.

The two drunks run off by Ogden from the bar had been shouting outside of the rail office, which had finally roused Harris up. Surly and ready for a fight, he opened his door roughly, staring hard at the two men. Harris had not shaved and he was sure he looked a little more wild than most were accustomed to.

"What the devil?" Harris demanded.

The two men, railroad by the look of them, looked startled to see the lieutenant, despite arguing in front of his door.

"Oh. Lieutenant!" The drunk was slurring and unsteady on his feet, but giving it his all to keep still. "We didn't…"

"What? Why are you carrying on like that?" Harris' tone was a might softer, but only just.

"We thought we were elsewheres. We weren't going to…"

"What's your name?" Harris asked.

"O'Malley," the younger of them answered, looking petrified, and unstable on his feet. "This here is Walker." Harris guessed they were likely still drunk from the previous night and was quickly losing any semblance of patience for this talk.

"O'Malley, then. Just speak up, son."

The other, slightly older by the looks of him, finally got some muster in him and spoke plainly. "We just want to know what's happening, sir. We've heard things, in the camp. Men are dying."

"The cold always gets some, but the blizzard has passed," Harris said simply, a crude and matter of fact tone in his words. This was not a conversation he wished to have and wanted them to move on as swiftly as possible.

"No… sir," O'Malley replied, his voice flattening and getting more sure, but quieter. "More than the cold. We've heard, some of them boys got kill'd, even that bastard on the main. Some… thing got 'em. We seen the blood, sir."

Harris thought carefully. A misstep here could lead to a riot, or desertion, especially with the blizzard passing and the snow clearing. Worst case, there could be violence with no sufficient force to protect the people. O'Malley and his friend seemed content to wait on his answer.

"I understand the rumors," Harris finally answered, conspiratorially. "There have been incidents." O'Malley's eyes widened and Walker looked satisfied a moment, that quickly turned to troubled concern. He seemed to realize being correct may be satisfying but it meant he was in danger. "I put it to you both, as men, to not let fear get the best of you."

Neither seemed to have anything to say, but their expressions hardened; a good sign. Harris drove the point and continued. "There is an animal, of some kind, and it is coming into our camp. I charge you both now." They both swelled in size, though it appeared comical as they swayed in their spot, like sleeping–walking children. "I want you both to sober up, get yourself coffee from the mess. I want you to gather as many able-bodied men as you can, anybody with a rifle, or a pistol. Get me a posse." Harris pointed down both ends of Hell Street, to the south at the tracks and the north to the plains. "As you get the men, have them make formations at each end. We're going to protect this town."

Both men nodded but neither moved. Harris buried his frustration and clapped both men on the shoulder. "I am entrusting this to you. Do not let me down, men. They're all counting on us. Go about it." With a final light push, both nodded and started for the mess tent, as instructed.

He waited a moment further, watching them depart. His sense of control was in serious jeopardy, and this conversation with those kids only brought the feeling to bear for him. Barnett would come back with some compliment; he could only with hope enough, and fast enough. Ahlborn had likely gone off to his death, but Harris could sleep with that thought.

The cold started to settle into his bones as he stood on his porch. He grabbed his coat and hat and set out about his day. Like so many, the smell and promise of breakfast lured him to the saloon. He would have to solve each problem as they came, after some food and coffee.

VIII

Abigail's was already getting busy by time the sun was up enough to fully light the sky. The two wood stoves were pumping as much heat as they could into the tent, and the sour smell of sweat and unwashed bodies made an unpleasant cloud in the tent, but nobody paid it any mind. Baths were nowhere to be found in this camp, in this cold.

At the bar, Abigail dropped two tin plates in front of two cowboys, who tucked heartily into their eggs and beans with a chunk of oven biscuit. As Harris approached, he could pick out the massive shape of Josiah Ogden, at the end of the bar, his usual haunt.

Harris regarded the veteran with an odd look. Despite the old man's continued willingness to lend his counsel, perhaps even help, Harris still felt some bitter sense of duty to keep some things from the man. He did not fully understand that instinct, he had been given nothing to suggest it was called for, but it was strongly imprinted in him. He truly wished it were not so. Their last talk had even been what Harris could call productive. He was short on friends, just now, and could use one.

Harris came to the side bar, remembering his manners and removing his hat. Ogden surely saw him but said nothing, lost in thoughts of his own with a cup of coffee between his fingers. Both men seemed content to wait in their silence, and many things were said in that silence. To an outsider, it could have even looked awkward, but neither felt it.

"Didn't sleep, didja?" Ogden asked, taking a long and slow sip of his coffee. Harris could smell the bitterness of it from where he stood but Ogden gave no sign he could taste it.

"No," Harris growled, clearing his throat. "Take it you didn't, either."

Ogden shook his head, slowly arching his back and stretching. He had been on that stool a moment too long. "No. Too much cold. Too much worry." Ogden turned now to look at Harris, that same piercing honest look he gave most things. "You feel it, lieutenant?"

"Feel what?"

Ogden sniffed loudly, tilting his head back to look up at the rippling top of the tent. "Couldn't tell ya, but something's gonna happen, real soon. The blizzard didn't stop it, from what I hear. Got what, four more?"

Harris nodded, looking around. Nobody was paying them any mind. "Four. For sure. Some from the cold."

"This thing is hungry. Ain't never heard of something like this. Even the nastiest of beasts stops when it's had its fill. And with the blizzard over, if your man's team don't get it, it's going to come here. We're just a feast to it, lieutenant." The old man's tone turned serious. "We don't kill it, many of us don't make it home, huh?"

Harris said nothing a long while. More men filed into the tent, in groups of two and three, all bundled tightly. One skinny man was wrapped in so many furs he looked like a buffalo on stilts, raucous and acting like an ass, disturbing the quiet of the tent, to Harris' annoyance.

"You could go," Harris said. "Snow's clear. You could be in Flagstaff by night, easy. Safe and sound."

"Aye, I could," Josiah said, "and I would be safe." He looked around disapprovingly, arching his back further and standing, in such a sudden movement it startled Harris to see the old man move so quickly. "Come on, I need some air."

IX

The air was crisp and bright, filling and burning lungs almost instantly. Despite the recent snowfall and storm, the air was dry and bitter, making skin ache and the mouth turn to sand. Josiah had his coat wrapped tightly around him as they exited the warmth of the tent, and both men found it bracing. The noise of the town had risen with minimal warmth of the sunlight, with many beating new paths in the already waning snow. The road, usually a rocky soft powder, was mixing with the snow to turn to a thick slosh of cold mud that stuck boots.

Neither spoke a moment, watching the movement, standing to the side to allow more into the saloon. To Harris' surprise, his message to O'Malley had gotten through and already a few men were carting materials to the rail line at the southern end of Hell Street, just to their left. Josiah seemed to notice, fishing his tobacco out of a deep coat pocket, he nodded curtly toward the affair.

"Defensible positions. Each end. This thing seems to favor them, might give us an advantage to have a firing line," Harris answered simply. Josiah said nothing, finishing his cigarette methodically and lighting it. It smelled stale and putrid, but the old man did not show he noticed or cared.

"Not a bad idea," Josiah finally said. "Should find

that boy, Moon. He's a shot and would help. He already winged it once, I'd reckon he'd like to mount this thing."

"I'd pay him for the trouble," Harris answered, with a hint of humor. He turned to the veteran with a hard, fixed stare. "We have to get this thing. We can't keep losing good men to this... whatever it is. Any more, and the camp will riot, or just desert."

"It'll ruin your railroad project," Josiah agreed, not making eye contact. "And you'd find yourself without a job."

Harris looked down at his feet, slowly pressing the surrounding snow down around him. "There are more important things, Ogden. I didn't used to think so, not even during the war. The cause, the victory, that's what mattered. Lives were just what was needed. Called for. Even my own, I thought. I'm as surprised as any that I made it through the war, thinking that way. I don't know, maybe I still think that, somewhere. Might always." He took a deep sigh, shuddering in the cold. "I may have just lost some conviction with it." This shocked Josiah and he finally turned and faced the junior officer.

"Well, alright, yankee. Let's get to killin' this thing, then."

Before either man could move on, Josiah noted a man riding hard down the main stretch. Even from so many yards away, Josiah could hear the beast strain and whine.

Such desperation worried Josiah and he moved his hand to his pistol, watching the rider bear right for the office. The horse stuck in the cold mud as it rapidly came to a stop just a few feet from the men.

Neither Harris nor Josiah recognized Decuir as he dismounted. He looked rough, his skin red and raw, wind burned and maybe a bit of early frost bite. "Lieutenant Harris," he finally said, his voice ragged, "I was one of those in the hunting party, with your man, Ahlborn. I am Decuir."

Harris' eyes lit up with recognition and were silenced half a moment later with realization. Harris spoke quietly and with precision. "Any others?"

Decuir was still catching his breath, his grip tight on the reigns of the panting beast he rode in on, a horrible noise it made, a dying sound. "Ahlborn sent me back, a couple were still fighting when I left. It ambushed us."

Josiah gave the lieutenant a grave look, his deeply lined face tightening in concern. None of them need say, their hunting party had never stood a chance, and they were now down that many potential fighters. Harris would not let on but the loss of Ahlborn hit him hard. He liked that man, he had potential, and was stalwart as any he had seen in the war.

"Ambushed? There was more than one?" Harris asked.

"No, just one. But it was so fast. It feinted, it tricked us. It knew how to avoid our guns."

Harris shook his head. "That's not possible."

Decuir spoke again after a spell, his voice finding its resolve. "I saw it, lieutenant. Properly saw it. It's no animal."

Harris took a moment to answer, with the same calculated pace. "What do you mean, it's not an animal? Even this man here has seen it, it's clearly a beast."

"A beast, may be, but it's no animal. Nothing to be found on this Earth. It may move like one, of sorts, but it thinks. Thinks like a man. I can't rightly explain it."

Josiah took note of that comment, putting himself more before the shaken Decuir. "I've seen this thing, chased it, even managed to hit it once. It's no man."

Decuir shook his head, his body quivering. "Surely is no man now, but I am telling you what I saw. It's... nothing of God's kingdom. A devil, if I could believe such things." Josiah shuffled his feet and considered to himself. Harris was at a loss for words. He was as godly a man as they came, but he had surely never seen a devil or demon at his doorstep. No matter its nature, it was flesh and bone and they could kill it.

Decuir would not answer any more, only shaking his head, still clutching the reigns of his protesting mount. His body, carried by whatever nerves he still possessed, was beginning to fail him, his shoulder slumping and his body withering, shaking now from cold and weariness.

"Decuir," Harris finally answered, "see to your mount, he looks done in. Get yourself warm. See a doctor. I appreciate your pains, I know it couldn't have been easy to leave like that." Decuir struggled to abide, moving ever slower. He seemed drunk, or delirious. Josiah had moved to the side to allow the man to pass, but as he took a feeble step into the melting snow, Decuir lurched forward, his strength having abandoned him.

Josiah grabbed the man quickly, stumbling to find his footing. Harris reached a hand out, but Josiah had a firm grip and was able to right him. "I'll get him to the surgery, lieutenant." Without a word, Josiah hefted Decuir onto his saddle like a sack of flour, taking his horse by its reigns, and dragging them both off down the lane.

Harris watched them go with mixed feelings. For the first time since he arrived, his thoughts now were no longer for the railroad or his project, but for the safety of not only himself but every man and woman in camp. If Decuir was right, and this thought like a man, the hunting party may have been enough to anger the beast and drive it to anger, and take lash out at the camp. To that point, the creature had seen fit to take one, or two, at a time. With determination, it could destroy the town, if they could not stand to it.

Drowning in his thoughts was not serving him or the

town, so he turned his attention to the fortification growing in front of his office.

X

It was not yet midday and the fortifications had taken shape. Within two hours, nearly the full width of the increasingly muddy lane, on both ends of town, was taken by a roughly curved wall, almost three feet tall, composed of crates, sacks, and drums, wrapped in barbed wire and various other items from town.

Throughout the building of the walls, a number of men had joined the effort, some at the asking of a sobering O'Malley, and some out of curiosity. At Harris' request, one of the storerooms at the heart of town had been opened and several men from the railroad security had taken rifles and ammunition from the stores. They now divided the rifles every couple feet across the fortifications, leaning them against the wall carefully. Between each sat a box of ammunition.

The relative quiet and mystery of events in town was now changing. While some of those quietly waiting out the delay in their camps had been only vaguely aware of some trouble with an animal, and a few others had remained entirely clueless, as they came onto the main stretch to see the defenses, news spread fast.

The reliability of what was happening degraded fast, causing some panic among those uninformed. Some of the camps on eastern end of town, furthest from the main camp, had heard of a disease spreading, causing many to load up their camp and leave town in great haste. Many of them were camp followers and their absence would not be noticed for some time.

Within the main drag, the more able and curious, bolstered by the slight warmth of the shining sun, were approaching the defense builders, asking questions. Gathering himself, the fully adorned Lieutenant Harris had taken position at the southern fortification, just a few yards back from the edge of the arroyo. No less than two dozen men were bundled and bunched, interested and worried.

Harris turned to the motley bunch, most railroad workers, with a couple followers, a hunter or two and even a prospector. They were a disparate group, but they were able and waiting. Rather than dismiss the opportunity, Harris seized upon a chance.

"Gather 'round!" Harris barked, his lungs burning from the sudden rush of cold. He waited for the attention to come to him. "We got ourselves a matter, and we need able men, willing to fight!"

"Is it the Indians?" One voice, old and cynical, rang out from the back of the group.

"No," Harris replied quickly. He chose his next

words carefully. As his voice had begun carrying, more and more had come out of the surrounding buildings, listening. "There is… an animal, something big, attacking the town. It has been here many times now, and we know it's going to come back. And we aim to kill it."

Grumbles from the assembled were lackluster and none immediately spoke up.

Frustrated, Harris climbed to the top of the fortification, not even two feet wide at its widest point. He drew himself to his full height, his head raised high. He took his wide hat and waved it over his head, like a commander marshaling his forces. He noted the young hunter, Moon, had taken a spot at the front of the assembled, just to his right.

"Hear me!" The man born of the war, the younger idealist who had earned his commission, could now be seen. The boss of the railroad was set aside and his place stood a soldier, proud and vigorous. "I know you're scared. Confused. Maybe you think this is not your battle!" Harris' voice rang sharp and true across the wide open of Hell Street, the steam of his breath shooting forth like from a canon. "But hear me when I say, this creature, it is unlike any other. It will come for you, for all of us, and it will kill all of us if we do not kill it first."

The murmuring of the crowd was louder now, excited, and full of fervor. Harris took a deep breath. "We are setting up barricades at both ends. Men, I have fought in a hundred battles, against thousands of men. I have beat death every time it came for me, and by god now is not when I die, not against this. We will kill it and mount its head on my door!" He raised both arms, looking like a preacher in the holy light of day. "Who's with me?!"

A great cheer rose from the dozens of men now assembled before him, all of them transfixed on the sight of their leader. Capitalizing on the momentum, he jumped down from his position, grabbing the nearest set rifle and handing it decisively to the man closest to him, pressing it into his chest until he grabbed it. There was a moment of hesitation between them, but the man simply nodded, gripping the rifle.

Harris turned to the waiting Moon, his own rifle slung over his shoulder. The young hunter had watched with attention and patience, a slight smile on his face.

"Hell of a speech, lieutenant."

Harris managed a small smile, nodding. "May have borrowed pieces from a Major I fought with in Tennessee." He motioned to the men and the rifles. "They may be eager, but I know many of them aren't shooters. Would you be willing to help drill them? I don't have enough of my security to do the job."

Moon's face went stern and he gave a curt tip of his head. "Leave it to me."

As Harris turned to take stock, a voice called out from the distance. "Lieutenant!"

Harris turned his attention to the voice, some yards down Hell Street, a man standing in the lane, waving down and pointing to the north end. Harris saw a posse of horses coming up the lane, a few dozen at least. Though he could not see the faces at this distance, he knew it could only be his cavalry.

XI

Barnett looked a little worse for wear, but his grim determination was a welcome sight to Harris. Behind him, his assembled group was taking in the town, some of them dismounting.

"I am glad to see you," Harris told Barnett, not bothering to hide his excitement. Barnett did not smile, but his expression softened, his usually neat appearance rough and disheveled. "Looks like you found some help."

Barnett drew his rifle and appraised his collection of men. "I was lucky. We have about three dozen. All shooters. There were only a few at the office from security I could pull." The men passed them by in groups of three or four at a time, heading into town. Barnett interrupted himself to turn back to the group, gesturing to the south. "You can stable your horses in the livery. Saloons are down the way, but stay sober!"

Neither spoke again for a time, letting the group disburse and find their way. Harris was not immediately impressed by what he saw, many of the men older, patched and worn. The ride could not have been easy on some of them. Many came with their own rifles, though the quality varied wildly. The hunters among them seemed to be faring better in appearance and materials.

Barnett turned back to Harris, dropping his voice. He turned the collar of his coat up against a new gust of wind. "We didn't have enough in the offices. I spoke with the marshal." Barnett tilted his head toward a larger group of men moving down the lane, all of them in heavy coats and moving carefully. Harris thought of wolves, watching them. "That's the so—called Dakota Reese Gang. Ruffians, really. According to the marshal, Dakota is just a two-bit con, but his men are dangerous. Offered them a deal to fight to get out of some trouble. They'll leave the county after, if they know what's good for them."

"Marshall chose not to come, I see." Harris' tone was mocking and venomous; he had expected some measure of concern from the law, but perhaps that was not to be found out in the west like it was in the more settled parts of the country.

Barnett scoffed jovially. "No, he thought it best to stay in town, it seems."

Harris nodded, continuing to watch the gang walk away until they had turned into one of the saloons along the lane. "Think they'll keep to it, this gang?"

Barnett scoffed, holding his arms tightly. The sun was still high but whatever warmth it could provide was waning fast, with a bitter wind kicking up from the west. It would be a cold night. "I told them whoever killed this thing would be famous. They liked that. I wager they'll like the fight. And the money."

Harris chuckled, gracing himself against another gust. "That'll do, I think."

A volley of shots from down the lane brought both men's attention, a series of pops ringing in the distance that echoed hollow down the shop fronts of Hell Street. Harris suspected that Moon had begun drilling. The irregularity of the shots showed their untrained nature. It had been some time since Harris walked men through drills, he thought he may benefit from the experience.

"I am going to go see about the southern camp. You stay here at the north. Get them fed, equipped, whatever is needed. Keep them assembled, keep them ready. That beast dies tonight."

XII

The fervor brought up in the camp throughout mid—

day diminished quickly as the weather turned. The snow stopped melting, though he skies remained mercifully clear, preventing any more snow fall. The wind had grown consistently, blowing strong at regular intervals.

As the sun started to wane, the cold rose fast and most of the idle and curious had already retreated. The more cautious had taken back to their camps, bundling down with their firearms or other makeshift weapons. The barber, Rookwell, had locked up his shop, barricading it as best as he could. He had retreated to the back of his shop, sitting on his straw bed with a double-barrel shotgun pointed and a bottle of whiskey in his hand. He had decided he would ride out whatever would happen, right from that spot.

Many more still had taken the choice to leave the camp all together. A proper count never did happen, but many that left were from the carry–ons, those that tried to profiteer most from the camp. Only a few from the railroad left, those too cowardly to wait out their wages. They told nobody they were leaving, taking only what little they could fit in a bedroll and riding off well before dusk. The camp, overall, was well–rid of them.

Whatever drills and practice had ended with the coming wind, with many retreating inside for as much warmth as could be managed. At the northern embankment, now fortified and looking quite like the sort seen in the war, Barnett had hunkered himself in as tightly as he could. Before setting up, he had ensured plenty of shots for his Sharp's rifle, now resting carefully on the top of the fortification. A few men had stayed with him even though it was not yet coming to night. They were all from the railroad's own security, good lads with the sand to take a post they did not fully comprehend, and Barnett was grateful for them.

The sun had begun to set ominously early, and most in town had taken notice. The only ones free of looking were those that had taken up in the saloons, drinking until the time they were called. Barnett and his men had finally given their eyes a reprieve, looking to the sky as it began to darken. Barnett sat still, passively, watching the sky turn to a pale blue, with arrows of marigold that came from over the peaks on the horizon. It took hardly no time for the sky to light red like fire, spreading from the west to the now growing black in the east.

At the southern encampment, Harris had taken a similar stance as Barnett had at the north. Like his friend, Harris was watching the sky, more able to see the sun set not quite over the vanishing rail line in the distance. With the dropping sun, the wind had died down enough to keep the worst of the cold off of them. The night had to come, Harris knew, and he had done everything within his power to prepare for this moment, but still he could only think of the things he still might have done.

As the final course of the sun sank below the distant mountains to the west, the sky was lit bright orange, a scalding color that could only make Harris smile. He had seen an endless number of sunsets in all of his years, all across the country and nothing had even come close to the beauty of the sunsets of the desert. He had secretly come to believe that this was God's parting gift to the last of the unsettled lands, the light of his glory as his creations chased after him. He was sure he would never again see such a brilliant sight.

XIII

Abigail's saloon was packed well past comfort. Seemingly every inch of the floor space had been taken by a rowdy assortment, with the only thing uniting them being a search for some measure for comfort.

For most of the railroad crew, they were merely looking for some heat. This was but the latest stop in their work, and there would be others, each with their own trials and dangers. This one too would soon be behind them and they tried not to linger on the point.

Most of the recruited fighters that had come in with Barnett had taken up on the other saloons along the strip, rougher places that rarely saw the railroad crews. Dakota's gang was an exception, having taken up a table near the bar, playing poker and drinking a shared bottle of whiskey that Abigail made them buy upfront. They had not caused any trouble, despite being louder than most of the others.

True to his nature, Josiah had once again taken his usual place at the bar, on the end. Instead of being alone, this time he had been joined by Moon. With his rifle between them, Moon had his hat off and was halfway through his second bowl of stew, fresh from Amos' kitchen in the back. He had not eaten properly for several days, and his young body was making up for lost time. Josiah had decided not to eat, despite urging from Abigail on the matter. His stomach was tied in knots and he could barely stomach his coffee.

He was uncertain of where his worry came from, exactly. There were dozens, hundreds, of guns now pointed at this creature, whatever or wherever it might be. He had no evidence, but he was sure it would be coming again tonight. If it had taken out that Pinkerton's hunting party only a few miles away the night before, it certainly could not be far, and this camp was certainly its only source of food in these hills.

If he could be certain of anything, Josiah knew in his bones that if they tried for this creature and did not put it down, they would likely not get another attempt at it. Whatever nerve that held this camp together, marshaled by the leadership of Harris, would break without success. The town would die, and possibly many people with it. Maybe himself, as well.

Dying was not the worst that could happen, he supposed. Dying in a fight with a creature straight from Hell itself seemed like a goodly sort of way to go, the kind he could be proud of. All the better than dying of rot and age. All the same, if he had his way, he would take the demon with him.

Moon noisily finished his stew, a wide look of satisfaction of his face. Josiah smiled. He remembered a time that a hearty meal would be all it took to bring him back from whatever edge he stood at.

"Better?" Josiah asked gruffly, taking a sip of his now cold coffee. It was bitter and awful, but he would finish it.

"Better," the young hunter agreed. He sat back, taking a deep breath. Moon now looked around the saloon, noticing for the first time just how busy it really was. "Quite a lot, isn't there?"

Josiah nodded, also turning to give the room his attention. A notable change, aside from the more varied sort of man on the floor, was that most now cradled a gun over their shoulder, at their knee, or tucked into a belt holster. Since coming to town, despite an absence of any gun ordinance, he had never seen so many armed.

"It could be good," Josiah agreed, his voice low and glum, belying his attempt at agreement. "But it could be dangerous. These men aren't fighters, even less are any kind of hunter. There are some veterans, maybe, but I don't see soldiers. A fool with a gun could do more damage than that creature."

Moon seemed disheartened with the opinion. The earnest and loyal nature of Moon, as naive as it was, could not think of a man doing anything other than his best. Josiah seemed to notice this and smiled disarmingly, clapping Moon strongly on his shoulder.

"Never you mind, Thomas," Josiah announced a little louder, his voice chopping at the surge of sound to be overheard in the din of the saloon. This was the first time Moon had been called such since leaving the farm some years before, and he did not think it was an accident. "You watch, many of these will break ranks when they really get a look at this thing. The only ones left to fight will be those that oughta."

When Josiah turned back to face the bar, he noticed Abigail watching him, her stern face twisted into a damned odd expression. Josiah looked at her for an answer, but whatever she had to say to the veteran she would not say in front of the hunter.

Josiah finished his coffee in one long take, grimacing as it went down. He held up two fingers to Abigail, his face still sour. Wordlessly, Abigail put down two shots in front of both men, with a third in front of her. She quickly filled them, with Josiah and she picking theirs up immediately. A nudge from Josiah got Moon to pick up his. Nary a word as all three toasted their coming trials.

XIV

The sky was a strong and clear black as the sun finally retreated. The moon was nearly half-full, casting a pale light that gave some small visibility. The cold, dry air was spared from the wind earlier in the day, and all was calm and quiet.

With the setting of the sun, more and more men had come out of the saloons and other nearby buildings, joining the encampments nearest them, with a stronger amount joining the northern camp, just at the edge of the main buildings leading to the road out of town. Lined up shoulder to shoulder, most of the men had taken to their back to the embankments, with a few look-outs on the line looking out into the dark.

On the northern camp, Barnett had more than a dozen men, some of them flanking the fortification at the edges, standing and kneeling against the false-fronts of the businesses. He knew a couple had taken to the camp tents themselves, peppered far beyond the edge of the camp. To his surprise, one of those with a rifle pointed out was de Soto. The young Spaniard, bandaged and still suffering from frostbite in his fingers, had merely asked for a rifle and to be pointed in the right way. He had said nothing further and only continued to watch.

XV

At the southern fortification, around twenty men had assembled, much the same as the northern encampment has done. As the town neared the southern fortification, more of the business fronts stood as sentry points, with many shooters camped in doorways and porches along the strip. The foreman, Brooks, had voluntarily set himself up in front of the railroad office, not far from the encampment itself. He had set an uncomfortable chair in front of the door, a Remington rifle across his lap, his heavy fur wrapped around himself. He had bled for this railroad, and all he could do was protect that legacy.

Harris continued to stand near the center of the fortification, straining his eyes to see out into the darkness beyond that hid the drop off into the canyon just a few yard ahead of them. He knew the waiting would exhaust his men but he found little alternative. This adversary moved fast and by time they could muster a proper defense, it could be gone. Thankfully, the men had taken to alternating between resting and watching on their own accord.

The quiet of the night was only broken by the occasional movement of wind and the muttering of the men. Some loud frivolity came from the saloons, but that could not be helped. At Harris' estimation, this may actually help draw in the beast, if it were not already sufficiently enticed.

Harris turned to the men around him. Half a dozen of them had guns pointed aimlessly out into the dark, the rest sitting in small groups, either talking among themselves or sitting quietly. One or two were sleeping lightly, still clutching their rifle barrels. At the far end, the young hunter Moon had taken up position. Harris was pleased to see Ogden had taken up position next to the boy. He was not sure what appealed the reb to the boy, but he was pleased to see it all the same.

Despite the tension, a fragile sort of peace fell on the men on watch. Harris had seen a hundred times before, a mixture of fear, doubt, determination, and some resignation. In the cold and dark, he could not tell which fit which man. The tension could be felt on every inch.

To spare his feet, Harris started walking down the length of his fortification, idly at first but continuing with more purpose as he saw Ogden watching him approach. Neither spoke for a moment, each watching out into the darkness. Moon took the opportunity to take a rest, sliding against the box he had been mounted on.

"Comfortable?" Harris asked him.

Moon heaved a sigh, smiling boyishly up at them.

"Who wouldn't be? This is like hunting a deer on ice. If the deer were hunting me back."

Harris chuckled. "All of this preparation. It had better show…"

Josiah scoffed loudly, fishing out his tobacco and leaning against the fortification, grunting loudly with the effort. The cold and damp was playing hell on his body and he felt stiff. "Oh, it's coming, lieutenant." Josiah finished rolling his cigarette, quite shoddily, and turned awkwardly in place, looking to the man rested next to Moon, who had been listening.

"You," Josiah barked. "What's your name?"

"Gabriel," the man spoke plainly. He offered nothing further, staring into the distance, seemingly lost in thoughts all his own.

"You one of the railroad workers?" Harris asked gently.

"Line splitter," he said simply.

"Ever killed anybody before?" Josiah asked him.

"No. I've never shot anything before." Gabriel's indifferent tone slipped into a cracking uncertainty. Harris had not understood the old man's intent, but now he saw. Gabriel, like so many more of them surely, was lost in their thoughts, thinking, wondering. They were afraid, more than Harris had realized.

Ogden heaved his large frame around, moving in

front of Gabriel, taking a rough knee in the snow, his massive body moving disjointedly, and though he spoke directly to him, the others around had no doubt they were being spoken to. Ogden spoke like nobody had ever heard in this camp.

"You afraid of dying? I have a secret for you. A secret I had killed many men and suffered to learn, so you hear you me, now. Death doesn't care for you. And he isn't after you. I know, because I have been after him for as long as I can remember and he ain't never shown up for me. What I reckon, death is a damned coward. He can't come for no man watching for him. He likes to sneak up on ya. So, you got death coming for you, and you look that son of a whore right in the eye and he will step right aside."

The tense calm that had befallen the men seemed to lift and all moved with a restless sort of energy. Josiah turned more purposefully down the line, taking to his feet with a renewed vigor. All eyes were on him now. "Remember! Right in his goddamn eye!"

The shouts from the other end came loud and fast.

XVI

"What did you see?" Barnett demanded.

One of his security men, Simon, had been the first to call out, pointing out. The half-moon light was enough to see the ground at forty feet with sharp eyes, but the utter darkness of the peaks on the horizon behind it made visibility poor.

"I saw it. Something moved!" Simon said hastily, shouldering his rifle.

"Nobody fire!" Barnett barked, raising his arms wide. "Hold!" Another voice called out, and then another, all down the line, each calling out some movement in the distance. Barnett spoke louder. "You're seeing ghosts! Now, quiet!"

Barnett turned his attention to Decuir, who had joined him a few moments prior. Barnett spoke direct and firmly to him. "You've seen this thing. What are we looking for?"

"It's going to come in low, fast. It moves in a back and forth motion. It'll look like just a gray shape, and it'll come right up on you, lead the shots." Decuir gripped his rifle tightly, his eyes fixed.

"You heard him! If you get a sight of it, you call out your shot but hold until you can hit it!" Barnett yelled. Decuir took a spot on the line near the end, his fist white as the snow around him.

Barnett's yelling had called out more men that had been tucked away in the shops and tents nearby, most cradling weapons, from rifles and pistols, to axes and shovels. All listened and waited, their eyes fixed at a shifting black of night that showed a hundred possible targets.

More footsteps came running from behind, but none of the men on the line moved, waiting. While most of the coming steps stopped short of the line, a smaller group, to the east of the fortification, continued on, moving confidently: Dakota Reese and his gang.

Barnett started to say something, but he caught himself. If these damned fool outlaws wanted to be bait, he would be all too happy to oblige them. They moved steadily, despite the shin-high snow, all with their weapons drawn. Dakota Reese himself was two paces out front of them, his pistol hanging lazily from his hand.

They managed twenty feet past the fortification before they stopped, forming a half circle, six in total, all looking around in different directions like they were waiting for bushwhackers. What minor talk there had been all stopped, with fingers on triggers. The world did not move.

XVII

Harris and those at the other camp waited. They could hear the faint shouts and the occasional snatch of conversation, but nothing could be understood. Nobody had fired yet, and that could only be a good sign at this point. The not knowing was unnerving the lieutenant.

Harris looked down the line, finding a young man he did not know among those leaning against the barricade.

"You!" His voice was commanding. The man stood at attention, full of energy and concern. "I want you to run down, get a report, and bring it back to us here. You're going to keep both sides informed. Understood?"

"Yes, sir!" He was off like a shot, moving as fast as he could in the muddy snow.

Harris faced the black of their own side. From what he had seen and heard of this creature, he would not put it past the thing to feint one side, only to attack the other. He did not wish to give much to flights of fantasy, but he had to believe the man, Decuir, that this thing thought like a man, and could attack like one.

"No matter what you hear, you keep your eyes to the canyon!" Harris shouted to his men, drawing his pistol. The silence that followed then was among the longest in his life. He could think only on his cold and sore body, his dry face, and stiff fingers.

Harris' discomfort ended with the first gunshot from the other camp.

XVIII

Dakota Reese, despite what his reputation would say of him, was not altogether a bad man. He had indeed been the first to see their adversary, a low slinking thing moving almost unnoticed to the left of the outlaw. Dakota raised his pistol, pushing one of his men to the side, away from the path of the thing.

He was able to get off two shots cleanly, but the smoke from the discharge made it hard to tell if his aim was true. His other men also aimed and fired, though they certainly could not have seen properly. Dakota ducked down, trying to see below the shot and gunsmoke, trying to keep his target in his sight. The Pinkerton had indeed convinced him he could achieve immortality if he was the one to stop the beast.

He could not see it any longer, and this brought his first round of genuine fear. The tales he had been told was of something never seen before, but this was truly something else. It moved so oddly, so fast. Dakota tried to listen but his men were too close, and too loud.

One of the gang had moved off from the main group, moving too aggressively, too blindly. He did not see the creature, which had moved behind one of the tent just to his right. In two strides, the creature closed the distance, its long arm grabbed the man by his leg, tugging him violently onto the ground. His chin came down hard, clamping his teeth down and severing the man's tongue cleanly, spilling blood onto the snow. He screamed fiercely as he was tugged by his ankle, getting dragged effortlessly. The creature tossed him roughly off to the side, several feet away, unconscious.

The rest of the gang fired, their shots wild and unfocused. Not a single shot made contact. The creature moved fast, its sweeping scuttle movement replaced with a single leap, throwing itself into two of the men, landing on top of them in the middle of the group. It swiped with both arms, tearing into the men violently.

Dakota had managed to avoid being jumped on, falling off to the side awkwardly. He spun onto his palms, trying to keep his eyes on the creature. Within seconds, his gang had fallen, their pistols empty or forgotten. Dakota dropped to his back, sticking his arm straight out and taking his last shot.

If his shot hit, the creature showed no sign of caring. Several shots rang out from the distance, ricocheting hollow off of the snow around them, and whipping past Dakota's head. The men at the fortification were firing, but they clearly could not see well or were trying to avoid the outlaw. While their shots were not hitting the creature, it was enough to keep it at bay. Dakota could only just make it out in the dark, moving slowly, its edges lost in the dark. He kept his gun leveled, despite being out of shots.

The gunfire paused long enough and the creature leaped again, landing firmly onto the exposed Dakota. He pulled a large hunting knife he kept at his belt, a gift from his father before he run off, and tried to take a swing. The creature easily grabbed his wrist in its large fingers, faster than he could watch, pushing Dakota's arm hard into the ground. Dakota felt his shoulder break as his arm came down, but he dared not scream.

The creature's other hand dug into his chest and stomach like so many knives, and how he screamed then.

XIX

Barnett had his Sharps rifle aimed but had not fired every shot he had. Reloading would be too slow and he did not want to waste a clean shot. A few had tried to shoot at the creature, but the outlaw gang had made it too hard to get a clean target. Just past his vision, he could hear the men scream, but there was nothing more he could do. Advancing on his own, in the dark, would surely be death.

It had been several minutes now and there was no more movement, no sound, and that bothered him more than the attack. He had no advantage or insight to what the creature may do, no knowledge of its habits. His hand began to ache, and his back strained, keeping his eye down the barrel of his rifle.

"Anything?" he shouted, hoping maybe somebody on the line had a sight on it. There were only low grumblings from the line, but nobody spoke up. He tried to suppress his frustration. Those damned outlaws had given away any advantage they had and now may have even tipped their hand, letting that creature pick off even more of them, too far away for them to be able to defend.

"To the right!" Decuir suddenly called out, far on that end of the fortification. Barnett moved fast, keeping his rifle loosely aimed to the north, to where the creature had attacked the gang. More and more men tore right, their rifles aimed, so far at nothing. To the right of the fortification was largely the pitched tent camps of the railroad workers, now dark and silent. All eyes kept to the right, searching for the adversary.

"Where?!" Barnett demanded, stepping to the edge of the line.

"I saw it!" Decuir said patiently, his own rifle raised. "Moving just between those tents. I think it's moving behind us. It's what it did before."

"Watch the flank!" Barnett shouted. More of the men from the left came over, some facing forward, some to the right. "You four!" Barnett pointed to some men from the center. "Watch the back, but don't hit the other camp! Watch your fire!"

Barnett held up a hand for quiet, but his men, with spent nerves, had lost any decorum, and were yelling among each other.

"Quiet!" Barnett yelled, for all the good it did him. Ranks broke, and the men started to scatter, each frantically pointing their weapons. Any ability to see or hear the beast was slipping, and Barnett started to truly panic for the first time.

Barnett turned sharply to the right at the sound of approaching feet, but it was only a runner, panting hard, moving rough through the snow. "What's happening?" the runner asked, his breath clinging tight, holding his chest. Barnett took a step to answer, but he was too late.

The runner had stopped between two of the slapdash shotgun buildings at the edge of the camp, and the creature had silently made its way between them. It had made no noise as it pounced, leaping no less than twenty feet, taking the runner fully off his feet, landing on top of him. Barnett had enough moonlight to see the creature pin the man down onto the muddy snow, its mouth digging violently into the runner's collar before he had fully fallen.

Barnett gave a startled yell and fired a shot, his long rifle barrel missing the creature widely. It paid him no mind a moment, taking a series of large bites out of the man, its strong jaws ripping and tearing with an awful sound that sickened Barnett. The runner continued to scream and flail uselessly, but his efforts were dropping rapidly.

He gathered his wits and took a moment to bring his rifle to bear, controlling his panic and breathing. He knew he had one shot, one chance to drop this creature, or he would be next. He was now only fifteen feet away, no more. The creature had no regarded the Pinkerton as a viable threat, it seemed, and that gave the agent the time he needed.

The shot took the creature hard at the shoulder, driving it off of the man. It gave a shriek, an unholy scream of alarm and hatred that shook Barnett. He had yet to hear the creature make a noise of any sort, to this point. It was unnatural, high and bitter, but bore a familiarity to it. The creature mewled and continued to shriek, rolling quickly in a thrashing ball, a sickening display that no animal would replicate. Its disjointed and long limbs flailing made Barnett think of a spider in its death throws.

His bewilderment at the creature's display stripped him of his memory to continue his shots. As he regained his composure, he readied his rifle with his final round, but was alarmed that the creature seemed to have similarly recovered, moving steadily on all fours, facing Barnett intently.

Barnett was now able to see the creature properly. As Decuir had told, the creature moved silently and quickly, its arms and legs long and spindled, unlike anything Barnett had ever encountered. Its body was lean and muscled, lithe, clearly that of a hunter. Barnett's true attention lie in the creature's face. By God's truth, the creature had a face like a man, its eyes cruel and sunken, sharp and shining. Its mouth held open with a monstrous jaw, filled with needle like teeth too big for its mouth, reflecting faintly a sickly yellow where not dripping in blood and offal.

Barnett heard the commotion of men behind him, but paid it no mind, planting his feat and readying his aim.

The creature seemed to know what the gun was, but made no effort to move, only staring down Barnett, swaying faintly in its place, each killer staring down the other and waiting for an opportunity.

The creature feinted a move to the left, with a sudden and deft movement that caught Barnett off guard. He over-corrected, turning his barrel and firing, but too wide. The creature moved swiftly, moving fiendishly toward him. Barnett gripped his rifle in both hands and swung it as the creature closed the distance, connecting the butt of the rifle with the side of the creature's head.

Unfortunately, bashing the creature was not enough to stop it, and it swiped its left arm wide, slashing Barnett broadly across his chest. He felt the numbing warmth of blood, but there was no pain yet. He swung his rifle again, in a wide circle, a desperation move. The creature dodged effortlessly, dipping below the swing and coming closer. It grabbed onto him and savagely bit into his side, and this time the pain was immediate and bright.

Barnett dropped to the ground, clubbing his fists down onto the smooth flesh of the creature's head. He turned to see a small huddle of men, no more than four, the only ones with the sand to remain, the rest having fled. They all had weapons aimed, including Decuir, but none dared to take a shot.

Barnett could not wrestle the creature free and he

felt his side continue to tear open, and he was getting cold quickly.

"Fire! Goddamn you, fire!" he shouted

XX

Harris had taken across the road as fast as he could, but the snow had not cleared as much in the middle of the way and his boots continued to stick into the mud. He was flanked quickly by Moon, who had followed wordlessly, and both men knew Josiah to be not far behind them.

They heard the shots and Harris had seen enough to curse the cowards who had broken ranks and run. He watched Barnett fall and tried to pick up his pace, wishing now for a horse. He was shocked then to hear a shot only two feet to his right. Moon had taken a knee and fired, apparently confident in his shot, but nothing had seemed to come from it.

It had taken only a minute to move from the sound of the first shot, but that was all it had taken. Within twenty feet of the fallen Barnett, Harris heard him to call for a volley and he could finally see enough for such an action. He knew there was no way to spare his friend from any gunfire, but he must have known his own survival was foregone and Harris had to trust him.

Harris fired his pistol, and many more shots followed,

from both sides. The creature let go of Barnett and both were peppered in bullets, each letting out screams of pain. The creature still not drop, turning from the larger volley of the men at the fortification and making its way toward Harris.

The lieutenant took aim and fired again, and the creature stumbled, howling in an increasingly strong scream of agitation, like any trapped animal. Shots continued to come from both sides, but the creature made no sign that he was impacted by them. Harris took a half step back, extending his arm for another shot when a sharp whistle followed a searing pain in his gut.

He dropped quickly, clutching his side. A wayward bullet caught him just under his rib. He had avoided being shot through the war and countless encounters with Indians, all to be hit by an errant bullet in this mining camp.

The creature quickly overtook him, bounding over him, trying to make its way out of the street and away from danger. Harris leaned back, his left hand clutching his wound, his right arm extended, shaking from the weight and effort of the gun, his eyesight swimming. He strained, holding his arm tight, and fired.

His bullet hit true, and the creature stumbled again, squealing loudly. It scampered back to its feet, a screeching wail following as it made its way between tents and vanished. Harris dropped his gun and all went dark.

XXI

"You should come with me," Josiah told Abigail.

Abigail had taken up position at the back of her saloon, seated near one of the stoves, with her girls around her, her double–barreled shotgun firmly across her lap. A couple dozen more people were seated in the saloon, but the noise and energy was quiet, severe. She saw the heavy face of the man and it concerned her. She had never seen him look so old, so worn, and strained.

Abigail rose quickly, never taking her eyes from his. She went to pass off her gun to one of the girls and Josiah held out a hand. "You should bring that."

Abigail's eyes widened in alarm. "I can't leave them—"

Josiah shook his head, growing impatient. "I brought Moon, he's going to sit in. Come on."

The street had become more active in the past few moments. Men, most of them armed, ran back and forth along the street. They walked out, side by side, to see several men carrying the limp lieutenant to his office. Abigail understood immediately and picked up her pace.

Josiah struggled to keep up. "Do what you can for him," Josiah told her, his breath ragged. He was panting, his body heaving. "I am going to stay out. This thing is going to come back."

"You didn't get it?" she asked. Her tone was a harsh condemnation and Josiah was reminded of his disappointed mother.

"We hit it. Several times. But it got away. It is very much alive. Keep that gun close." Before Abigail could say more, Josiah had walked off.

As she neared the office door, she noted Brooks in his chair, just to the side, still wrapped in his furs. She noted how shocked he looked, but paid him little more mind. As she tried to enter, a man left quickly, toward the surgery, likely for the doctor. Abigail entered the room quietly to see Harris on his bed, his coat and shirt off, aided by one of the workers. The other was feeding the stove, quickly warming the room.

Harris was mostly unconscious, groaning and sweating. Abigail could see his wound, a single hole in his gut; it was not bleeding more than a trickle, which she took as a good sign, for all she knew of gunshots. There was nothing more to do in the moment to help but wait. And wait she would. For as long as was needed.

XXII

The town had an eerily quiet hustle.

Josiah had made no effort to move overly fast and he surveyed his surroundings closely. He kept his gun in his hand, if only to help his balance. His chest burned and his back ached, making movement difficult and painful, but move he would. He passed the surgeon, bag in hand, running past Josiah as fast as he could toward Harris.

Harris was a strong man, tough as iron and twice as hard, but Josiah worried. A town like this, his chance of fever was high, and they were too far for any help. Live or die, Harris had done all Josiah could expect of the man, and wished him only well. If anybody ever deserved a chance to live, it was Jonathon Harris; a man of vision and purpose.

Many more men busied themselves, running hither and yon, some armed, and some just moving, a nervous sort of need. Josiah has seen it before in the war, especially just before and after a battle, that need to do something with the nerves. There is nothing else to do, really, Josiah assumed, though he wished the men would do something more productive, keep their eyes on the horizon.

Halfway up the town, the chest burning had subsided but his back pain spread, running down his leg, increasing his limp. How he hated this old, broken body, he just needed it to hold on this one more night, to stay useful. Stay lethal. After tonight, the beast would die, or he, and it would be on the others to finish the hunt if he did not.

As he got away from the center of town, the bustle of movement slowed, and quieted. He could feel the baited breath of many men around him, but at least he could not see them, the cowards, hiding from the devil and the cold in their tents. The northern fortification was quiet, and still, and Josiah could hear only soft wind across the snow.

Josiah was surprised to hear movement and he raised his Dragoon pistol, but it was not the monster, just a gray-haired man a little younger than Josiah, squat and moving quick on his feet, cradling a rifle. Josiah realized the man had been standing watch, quiet.

"Thought you were that thing," Josiah said quietly, lowering his gun.

Decuir nodded solemnly, his rifle at bear, his hands as white as the snow beneath him. He said nothing, looking about him, his eyes darting left and right, body twitching. Josiah became increasingly nervous, watching this man unravel.

"Were you here when it attacked?" Josiah asked, moving to the side, keeping a level eye on the man's gun.

"I was. Twice."

Josiah cocked an eye, grunting as he shifted on his feet. "Twice?"

"I went out with that Pinkerton, Ahlborn. We tried to hunt it." Decuir coughed, and Josiah saw it for the mask it was, hiding his fear, his emotion. "It hunted us. We were so easy, so helpless. We shoot it, and it carries on. Two times, I fail to kill it. I have hunted the biggest and meanest animals in this country, and this... It was too much. I don't think we can kill it."

"It bleeds, it fears. It can die," Josiah said simply. "What's your name?"

"Decuir."

Josiah moved closer, carefully. "Decuir. That's a different sort of name. You're still alive, ain't ya? So am I. Others, too, just over there." He pointed down the way. "Many of them can't fight. But, we can. You know, we all told each other, and ourselves, why we fought. It's getting on in years, now, and I know I had reasons I told people, what I told my wife." He took a deep breath, and he found it hurt, came up short, but it was enough. He continued.

"But really, it was all for my wife. She couldn't fight, not there, but I could. I could save her. I would fight for her. Everything else was a lie. I haven't had anything worth fighting for, until now. And it's not these people." That caught Decuir off guard.

"What then?"

Josiah leaned in close, and he was pleased to see Decuir looking terrified. "I don't care what you believe, but that thing is nothing less than evil, a demon sent up from Hell, and if I can be sure of any damn thing, it is that holy God Himself would have us kill this. Call it fate, or luck, whatever you like, but I don't plan to let God down."

Decuir said nothing, his eyes cast down the quiet, dark street. Lights of fire bobbed in and out, flickers of yellow and orange in the black. "Yes," was all Decuir could say. Josiah relaxed a little, leaning against the fortification, looking about him.

"Good man. That other Pinkerton. He was here, right?"

Decuir nodded. "It got him. Some others, too. They're still out there." Decuir pointed out into the dark, beyond the edge of the town. "I don't want to go out there, while it's dark."

"No, I wouldn't do that, either. What about the Pinkerton?"

Decuir sniffed, rubbing the back of his neck. "I moved him. It didn't seem right to leave him, like that. I pulled him, over there. I thought I'd bury him, when it was safe."

Josiah nodded. "Too right. I will help you."

Decuir was surprised, yet again.

XXIII

Harris had lost a lot blood by the time the surgeon finished and the air was still thick with the smell of it. The surgeon had been successful in removing the bullet, and had Harris stitched. The once clean hole was a black and red mess, crossed with dark silk stitches. Harris was bandaged and had passed out some time before.

Everyone else had cleared out, leaving only Abigail with him. She spent the time trying her best to clean up the spilled blood, though she had to admit her efforts were lackluster. It was still too cold to fetch water that would not freeze, and she was not willing to leave the lieutenant.

She was as surprised as any at how attached she had become to the man, in such a short amount of time. He was certainly old enough to be her father, but she had to admit the affection felt nothing like a father, nothing like she had felt with Josiah. She imagined his ways appealed to her, the sort of man to take a stand and do what needed doing, simply because it was so. She had not many such men in her life, and so few lived up to even a half-measure of a man like Harris.

So, the least she could do now was clean up and care for him. His skin was pale and he looked thin, sweating, despite the cold. It seemed like the fever was setting in, putting his future likely in the hands of God. She hated the idea that he was dropped and possibly die because of a fool's bullet. If she ended up having her way, she would see him beaten in the street for his mistake.

"You know," she said softly, looking at Harris' gently rising chest, "I didn't think much of you when you came in. Just another man, the next in thousands, come to this line. I've seen so many. But there was something different 'bout you." She paused for a time, just watching. She doubted very much that he could hear a word she said, but it seemed appropriate to share her thoughts with him now. It could not hurt anything now.

She continued. "Most men, they come out here hidin', or just taking what they can. Watching the world pass them by. No care for what more there is. But you… You see what can be. I don't see men like that out here. You care. I like that." She gently touched his arm but if he noticed, he gave no sign. "I do hope you recover."

The cabin was relatively warm now and quiet, which suited Abigail just fine. After the craziness of the night, she could use the peace. She worried about her girls, but that boy Moon seemed capable and tried not to spare more thought than she needed to. She was resenting her inability to do more for the cause, to protect the town. She was not defenseless, but she was no fighter, like the others.

The door opened quietly behind her, startling her out of her thoughts. Brooks peaked his head in, a strong cold wind cutting through the warm air unpleasantly. She relaxed a little when she recognized the foreman, but was annoyed with him all the same. She threw a blanket over the ever-shivering Harris.

"What is it?" she barked.

"Sorry, Abigail, got a word. They're sending some men out after the thing, and it's got people nervous. Got some unsettled folk in your place, and I thought you might want to be back in the saloon."

"Hell," she grumbled, looking to Harris. He was resting, it seemed, if a little fitfully. She admitted there was little she could do for him now, in this state. There were others that needed her, if only to keep the nerves in a check. Maybe a shot of bourbon was called for. "Right," she told Brooks. "I will head back over."

XXIV

Moon had not minded sitting with the women and drunks at the saloon, but as more time passed, his youthful drive for action overcoming any good sense of reason. Once Abigail returned, dismissing him, he could only think to wander the dark street of the camp.

His rifle held tightly in front of him, he walked aimlessly through the increasingly trodden snow, now little more than cold mud through the main street. His feet were sore and his head ached, but he found that mattered little. Up to this point, he had seen this event as a hunt, something to accomplish. But now, he was angry. Angry at the loss of such life, angry at the impossible nature of this creature, and, most of all, angry at his own failure to kill it.

It took him little time to wander into the middle of Hell Street, lit only by the faintest of moonlight. A few men moved about on either side of the street, most of them armed, half of them drunk. Moon found himself angry with them as well, though he knew this to be unfair thought. They had not failed any less than he.

At the edge of the street, the snow had not yet melted and smashed into the mud, and Moon was able to pick up a track. The foot print, clearly made by the creature, was almost like that of a man, but longer, almost twice as long, narrow, with clear claw imprints. It was the strangest track Moon had ever seen. He idly started following the tracks.

He was sure nothing would come of it, disappearing into the dark wilderness he would dare not venture, but it gave him a sort of purpose to look. The snow was thicker now and movement slow, but Moon was determined.

XXV

Dawn was not too far off now, and the cold was worsening. The air remained bitter, dry, and biting. As the sun came closer to rising, the wind would soon follow, but for now it remained blissfully absent.

The excitement of the earlier events with the beast had all but dropped. Nearly all of the armed men who had prepared to fight were now defeated by time, tucked away to sleep, or in a drunken stupor in one of the saloons. The camp was as quiet and barren as it ever would be.

Brooks, for his part, was a good and loyal man and

had remained on point in the front of the railroad office for hours now. He was no gunfighter, only a simple working man, and had no real personal connection to Lieutenant Harris, but as with Abigail, he admired the man, and respected his station. He felt a loyalty to the railroad, to his work, to his men.

But even Brooks had to admit there was a limit to his grit and he was drifting. His body and nerves were both exhausted. The cold had sapped his strength and despite his efforts, his hands were not working all that well any longer. He needed rest and warmth.

The light from the saloon was a warm glow and it would give him what he needed. A cup of coffee and some food, and he could resume his post, or find another to take his place. Most of the workers still asleep would be waking up before long.

XXVI

As Moon had predicted, the tracks had proven relatively easy to follow, but merely curved up through the edges of the camp until it ended at the lip of the arroyo. The thing must have dropped down into the canyon and gone off to wherever it goes. He reckoned its nest could not be far from the camp, likely somewhere in the canyon itself.

Despite expecting what he discovered, Moon still

found himself disappointed. The damned monster seemed to mock their attempts to confront it, managing to move through any harm, and escape easily. For the first time since it showed up, Moon gave serious thought at leaving the camp. Maybe even at first light, as that seemed to be the only thing the beast could not bear.

As relieving as the thought was, Moon was no coward and he would not flee, especially if Josiah was remaining; the young hunter would not want the veteran to think less of him. He did not find it likely the old man would leave while there was still a fight to be had. Whether that was brave or foolish was not for him to decide.

Defeated and playing with fate, Moon decided to follow the edge of the canyon until he reached the rail line to follow back to camp. Maybe he would catch some sleep before dawn, while they decided what the best option was. The snow was clearing, maybe they could get some people out now.

Moon was careful to stay several steps from the dark of the canyon, moving slowly, his eyes at his feet, as the night around him was entirely too dark to do any good. Almost twenty yards from the rail line, just now coming into view, Moon stopped cold.

The tracks resumed, but coming straight up from the edge of the canyon, as though the thing had dipped down and came back up elsewhere, covering its movements.

The tracks led straight back toward the center of town. The damned thing had not left, it was going to come up right behind them. Moon took to a run, immediately feeling the burn in his lungs.

He could not know how long it had been since the creature had gone back, and his panic set in. He may already be too late. He pointed his rifle into the air and fired a shot over the rail, away from the town. Maybe it would rouse people's attention.

He had to try.

XXVII

Josiah Ogden heard the shot, clear as day.

He had been ambling back toward Abigail's, gripped by the same desire as Brooks, for some warmth and food. His left knee ached and his chest felt heavy. It had been years since he had pushed himself so far, physically, and he felt it all weight on him. The shot took him out of his thoughts, and he disregarded all further concern for his body. He drew his heavy pistol and ran as best as he could through the mud of the street. He saw several others running out, somewhat timidly, from several of the buildings around.

They clustered aimlessly at the main crossroads, weapons raised, looking around nervously. Josiah stood outside of them, trying his best to keep his wits about him.

The men muttered and yelled about, chasing ghosts, and their own fear.

"Quiet!" Josiah bellowed, his head and gun both raised high. Not all heeded him, but enough did that he was able to hear better. From the direction of the tracks, Josiah saw Moon running flat out toward them. Josiah did not need to see his face to see the fear in the young man, moving quickly to meet him and close the distance.

"The tracks," Moon managed. His breath was all but gone and he struggle to keep his hands from shaking. Josiah tried his best to give the boy the time he needed to get his words. "They double back. I lost them in the mud, just outside town. It's here. Somewhere." Moon fell into a coughing fit.

Josiah picked up his head and listened, trying his best to shut out the rabble of the mass behind him. He knew they were in danger, and the confusion and noise they were creating would make things harder for them.

"Why would it fake leaving just to come back?" Moon asked, more to himself. He had gathered himself, though still a might short of breath. He stood next to Josiah, looking around sharply. Josiah had no answers for the boy. Nothing about this made sense to either man.

"We could check each building, see if we can find it," Moon finally suggested.

Josiah shook his head. "We need to stay together.

Even in groups, this thing is a danger to us. The more people we have, the better our chances. We would do best to stay in the open." Moon saw the wisdom of this and settled in for what he was sure would be a tense time until dawn.

Primal screams echoed through the streets, causing all heads to turn. Josiah started moving immediately, pushing his body with all of his might, with moon right at his back. "The railroad office!" he hollered. It did not take him long to close the distance.

XXVIII

Josiah could smell it long before he saw it. The smell of death came out strong from the small railroad office, wafting hot and sickly into the cold air. He did not pause, throwing his weight into the flimsy door of the building, knocking it clear of its frame. The blood was immediate and rank.

As the door flew back into the office, it clattered loudly against the stove in the corner, and it caused the creature to jump, startled. It had clearly burst through the office window, glass spread throughout the office. By the fire of the stove and the lantern on the desk, Josiah could see the creature had perched itself over Lieutenant Harris' bed, and it had dug violently into his chest and stomach.

The creature turned and snarled viciously to Josiah,

its body covered in the blood of the lieutenant, dripping blood and flesh from its fangs. Josiah was immediately horrified, disgusted, and wrathful. The man was clearly dead, ripped to shreds in a defenseless state. It felt like an insult.

Josiah raised his pistol and fired two shots rapidly. One just missed the creature's left chest as it anticipated him, but the second shot found solid purchase in the creature's gut. It squealed in pain, thrashing its long arms wildly within the small space. The scrape of claws on wood mixed with the creature's mewling howl could be heard far outside of the office building, but it did nothing to wayside Josiah. The old man shouted in response, his very soul and hate in every sound, a great primal roar. His face contorted and he felt the heat rise in his cheeks, his neck and chest straining. His breath caught, but he would not be stopped. He fired a third shot, which did little more than deafen him.

Moon had tried his best to set up a shot behind Josiah but the man's large body took up too much space. He moved around quickly to the now shattered window from the side of the building, trying for a shot. The creature had clearly been injured, its gut wound a black and festering spot that oozed a dark ichor, but it was not stopped. It gathered itself quickly, crouching into a springing position.

Moon pushed the long barrel of his rifle into the window and fired a shot. The great sound of the gunshot caused both the creature and Josiah to recoil, filling the small building with acrid smoke. The creature was interrupted, even dazed perhaps. Josiah held his breath as best he could, steadying his arm. He fired another shot, dead in the creature's chest.

The shot tore into the thin muscle of the creature's ribs, causing it again to recoil. For the first time, Josiah could see the creature properly. While it was clearly no sort of person, the way it curled into a fetal position, cradling its own body in pain and fear, Josiah could see this thing may have been a person at one time. Its breath, heard now for the first time, had become ragged and rasping, not unlike Josiah on a strain. Whatever the creature may be, or have been, he would see it killed.

Josiah aimed his pistol again. He knew he was low on bullets and could not afford to miss. He was careful. As he squeezed the trigger, the creature jumped up from its spot, playing possum. Josiah yelled in surprise and anger, the creature's wide arm swept up, knocking his gun to the roof and the shot went off.

The desk near the door had been saved the violence, and Josiah reached out to grab the lantern's handle, swinging it wide to the advancing monster. It stood now at its full height on its legs, shrieking and recoiling from the swinging fire. It was afraid.

Josiah took his chance. He knew if the creature could

recover, it could easily overtake him, like it had the others. It had already killed Harris and many more would die if he could not stop it here and now. Josiah spun the lantern overhand, throwing it into the creature.

The lantern crashed and splintered, and the oil ignited almost immediately. The creature fell back, scrambling wildly and scraping at its own flesh, trying to bat away the flames. Josiah jumped back, staying near the door. His pistol had a shot remaining and he wanted to keep it ready, in case it charged.

The creature landed into the wall opposite the window, shrieking and mewling a high-pitched scream, the enflamed oil creeping down its back and chest. It swung widely with its armed, blindly looking for purchase, a panicked reaction. From the window, Moon had repositioned and fired another shot, but neither man could tell if it connected, as the creature scream incessantly.

Moon readied another shot but before he could fire, the creature launched off of the wall toward the window. The top half of the creature hung on the frame, knocking Moon back. The fire was beginning to subside, showing only singed flesh. The smell was profound. The creature stumbled as it attempted to scramble out of the too–narrow window and Josiah fired his last shot. He saw the bullet catch the creature in its hip, tearing large chunks of flesh and black-ened–blood from its body.

The creature bellowed a louder roar of pain and fear, finally managing to fit its long limbs through the frame. Moon watched it land awkwardly just a few feet from him, and immediately it started to scamper from the office building. It moved slower than it had before, but still faster than any man could easily manage.

Moon was quickly after it. Despite being injured and in retreat, the creature was clever enough to not run in a straight line, choosing instead to dart from the left and right, a random and disjointed larp. Moon dared not try for a running shot, but he would if the creature stopped long enough to give him the chance.

As the creature neared the edge of the canyon, Moon hoped for a delay, a hesitation of any kind. Instead, the creature was only two feet from the edge when it leaped over the edge, throwing itself headlong into the slope. By the time Moon carefully approached the edge, he saw the creature had ended up in the bottom. Its sickly gray skin was scarcely visible against the fading snow in the base of the canyon. He watched the thing move south and he lost sight quickly.

XXIX

Any semblance of the fire was put out within moments. Aside from a horrendous smell of burning flesh and some soot on the walls, the building was no worse for wear. The same could not be said for Harris.

As Moon chased the fleeing monster, the assembled men in the road, who had been content to watch to that moment, rushed in. Josiah cleared the doorway for them, leaning against the wall outside, trying to catch his breath. His breathing had been getting steadily worse, and he wondered if now was the moment his heart would stop.

Wouldn't be the worst thing, he reckoned. The creature was certainly injured, more so than it had been up to that point. It may die, but even if not, it was likely that it would be too injured, or scared, to make any attempts on the camp again. It was not a complete victory, but it would suffice.

As the movement slowed and the men shuffled out of the ruined office, Josiah could feel air in his lungs again. The tightness in his chest loosened and the pain crept back down his back. He still had some life left, it seemed. For all the good it might do the man.

After the men cleared, it was Brooks that approached the building. He paid no attention to Josiah, walking slowly to the doorway. His stern and flat face betrayed little feeling, but Josiah could guess as to his thoughts.

"It came in through the window. We were here in seconds. He never stood a chance. You couldn't have saved him," Josiah reassured. His breath was becoming less ragged but the talking hurt.

"I left him. I was guarding him and I left," Brooks said plainly.

Josiah coughed violently, and straightened himself, but said nothing further. The cold was pushing itself back into his bones and he tried to fight it back. The commotion had brought even more from their buildings and tents, some only waking now for the first time. Dawn was not far off, now, the faintest of a glow peaking to the ranges far in the east. Many crowded now to the office, most unsure of what has transpired. Josiah paid none of them any mind until he saw Abigail approaching.

He moved quickly, intercepting halfway through the street.

"Is it true?" she demanded. There was no hysteria in her voice, only a determination and surety. Josiah could not reach her eyes and could say nothing. A simple acknowledgment felt a half measure. She took the truth from his silence and made no movement.

Moon had returned at that time, and his face was different. Still the youth Josiah knew him to be, there was a pall over his eyes now, a hardness. A hatred. He wordlessly walked up to Josiah and Abigail, his rifle gripped tightly.

"It's in the canyon. It's moving slow, its severely injured. It went south," Moon said. It was a challenge, framed in information.

Josiah knew the point and he was not going to argue. He turned to Abigail, who had a similar look to her face as Moon, and softly gripped her shoulders, meeting her eyes. As they connected, her stern resolve started to cracked and he shook her. "Stop. I need you to see to this lot. Work with Brooks, there. You and he are the last kind of leadership. Take care of Harris." Abigail's eyes swelled. "See to him, and the others. They deserve that. We are going to go get it." Abigail looked scared then, her body tensing. It was clear she did not want Josiah to be lost.

"No, you can't—" she started.

"Harris. And the others. It killed them, and now its injured. Harris gave us the chance. We're going to go finish it. Do as you're told." Nothing in Josiah's tone gave room for doubt or argument and he started walking away before any more could be said. Moon followed wordlessly.

Both men moved west, toward the canyon, both taking the time to reload. Neither shared their thoughts with each other, but nothing needed to be confirmed; they would come back with the thing's head or they would not come back at all. Before they could get much further, they heard a voice behind them.

"Wait!"

Moon did not stop but Josiah did. Decuir was fast approaching, his rifle at the ready, a lantern in his off hand. He opened his mouth to speak, but Josiah only turned back and continued walking. Decuir took the silence in stride and the three men started their descent into hell as silent avengers.

XXX

The slope into the canyon was loose and steeper than it had seemed. The lantern Decuir had brought brought little light in such a wide space and more than once the loose granite rocks of the canyon gave understep. Despite the slow movement, the three never lost patience.

The glow to the east was more pronounced now, a pale blue-white now pushing the black aside. As soon as Josiah reached the bottom, the last to do so, none of them could see the horizon any longer. The three look around them carefully before Moon started for the south.

The majority of the snow had yet to melt in the canyon, and what had melted from the sides had run into the bottom, turning the soft sand into a thick quagmire of loose mud. Their boots sunk through the snow into the mud and made for slow movement.

"Look," Deuir said suddenly, his voice low. They had passed under the foundation of the bridge and found the first tracks. Sprinkled around and between the tracks in the snow was a black trail of its blood. It smelled of death and reminded Josiah of mining run off. "It's still bleeding."

"Good," was all Josiah said. They continued, with Decuir in the front. The lantern hung from the end of his rifle, lifted only a foot from the ground. In the deepness of the canyon, the wind from the plains could not reach them and they passed in an eerie quiet stillness.

The canyon ran in a southwest direction, but started to wind wildly to the northeast and back before continuing to the south. The path was dizzying and disorienting and they began to grow concerned. The canyon went for too many miles and there was no telling how far their adversary could, or would, go.

"How far do we go?" Decuir asked. He was careful to make sure his meaning was not missed, as he would go as far as needed. Moon was the one to answer.

"Until it's dead. It can't go far, injured like this. The sun is coming, and it doesn't seem to like that. It'll go somewhere to hide and recover."

"Watch the tracks," Josiah answered, keeping up the pace from the rear. "There's probably divots or caves in the sides. It'll be in the first one. I doubt it'll be too far."

The narrow sky above the canyon was starting to show a glow and made seeing easier. Their pace quickened in the increasing light and they moved further to the edge of the canyon floor, out of the mud. All three could now see the clear tracks in the ground and followed easily.

Less than a mile from the bridge, after numerous

bends, the tracks and blood turned abruptly to the right bank. It took the men no time at all to find a thin cutout of the canyon, barely four feet high, slowing up as it went deeper. Without the tracks, it would have been overlooked easily.

The cutout appeared to be carved by water, and was only about seven feet deep. Decuir pushed the lantern into the space and immediately they could see the creature. Without hesitating, Josiah grabbed the lantern from Decuir, ducked down, and drew his pistol, leveling it at the creature. It made no attempts to move that he could see.

Moon was immediately behind Josiah, both with their weapons drawn. There was no room for Decuir, who waited outside, right at the edge. Josiah took a step, pushing the lantern and pistol closer. In the smaller space, the lantern lit the scene perfectly.

The creature was lying against the furthest corner it could. It was stretched on its back, its limbs splayed out. The burnt skin of its body was black and crept all over its body, clearly visible where the oil had dropped down its body. Blood continued to drip from its wounds, puddling shallowly underneath. The creature's chest was heaving and Josiah could hear its wheezing, labored breaths. It made a pitiful noise.

Despite their advancements, the creature made no attempts to move, to defend itself. Josiah wondered now what to do. He was not sure gunfire would kill it, given the number of bullets it had taken to that point. In this space, should the creature decide to fight back, they would be defenseless. Moon readied his rifle, thinking Josiah had lost his nerve, but Josiah reached up and lowered the barrel.

The creature followed them with its eyes, scarcely moving. It continued its labored breathing, its body continuing to struggle. Moon had yet to get such a clear look at the creature's appearance and it revolted him. It looked nothing more than a contorted and evil perversion of a man, twisted and lengthened. Its hairless body was tight and slick looking. Disgusting.

"I can't miss from here," Moon growled, trying still to raise his rifle barrel.

"You won't miss. But it might not kill it," Josiah whispered. He had to consider. He found it odd that this creature, so clearly driven by instinct and survival, would sit here now, doing nothing in the face of such danger. "Give me your knife."

Moon instantly pulled out a large buck knife from his belt and passed it. The creature eyed the knife and its breathing quickened, its movements shifting, but still it laid against the wall. Josiah held up the knife and watched the creature's beady eyes follow it. Its breathing changed, and its body stiffened. It may not have considered the guns a threat, but it certainly was fearful of the knife. Josiah slowly slid his pistol back into his holster, but those eyes were ever on the knife.

"Don't. Fire," Josiah breathed. Before Moon could guess what he was meaning, both he and the creature lunged at each other. Moon fell back, knocking his head into the low rock ceiling.

Josiah's larger mass won in the lunge, forcing the creature back into the corner. In the confined space, the creature's longer and stronger limbs could not get full motion, hindering its defense. The thing snarled and hissed at Josiah, its great jaws snapping uselessly, its too-large teeth not able to fit in its mouth, limiting its motion and ability to bite. Josiah punched the thing's face, just to the side of its jaw, knocking it to the side, stunning it.

Josiah seized his moment and grabbed the knife in both hands, driving it down into the creature's chest. The knife penetrated easily, burying to the hilt of the handle, and Josiah felt something inside give under the pressure. The creature's jaw widened and it shrieked loudly, a piercing and violent sound. A steady stream of the thing's thick black blood poured from the wound.

The creature fell back, its limbs twitching, and its breathing becoming increasingly shallow. Josiah sat back, leaning against the wall of the cave, watching its chest move less and less until it stopped entirely. A final, pitiful whine came from the creature and it was still.

"Is it dead?" Moon asked, a harsh tone in his voice.

Josiah nodded, coughing. His chest hurt and his vision swam in and out. He found it difficult to focus and breathing was taking more effort. But despite all of it, he was able to relish his triumph. Harris did not need to die, but this creature had decided otherwise.

"It's dead," Josiah wheezed, chuckling humorlessly. A flash of light startled both men, and they turned to see the start of golden sunlight hitting the walls of the canyon. Josiah smiled, watching the light for a time. "Do me a favor," he finished.

"What is it?" Moon asked. He was becoming alarmed.

"Take this thing out. Have Decuir help you. Burn it. Make sure nothing remains of it."

"Of course. Come on, let's get out of here."

Josiah only sighed. "I don't think I am." His voice was getting quiet and he could not raise it.

"What? Are you hurt?" Moon asked, looking for a wound.

"No," Josiah said easily. He was starting to feel loose, easy. He doubted that was good for him, but the pain was going away. He had not felt so little pain in years. He had forgotten. "I'm stayin'."

Moon suddenly understood and that hardened, hateful look was lost. He was again the same young man, from before all the death and evil he had confronted. "Let me get you help," Moon offered.

"Leave me. Burn that. Live." Josiah smiled broadly, the first time he could recall doing so. He felt lighter now. It was okay. All of it. They would live and there was nothing more to fight.

Then he finally found it.

XXXI

The morning was almost spent by the time Decuir and Moon climbed back up the embankment to the camp.

As far as Moon could tell, the town did not look or behave any differently from any other day. People made their way back and forth across the street. The railroad office was closed and looked no different than normal, other than the window being boarded.

In the road of the town, just off of the office, a wagon sat, with some bundles in the back. Brooks appeared to be tending to it, with Abigail close by, watching carefully. Moon approached Brooks. His rifle felt heavy in his hands and his eyes begged to rest. Brooks saw him and his eyes dropped. Abigail gave no sign.

"You're back," Brooks said dumbly. Moon nodded. Decuir stood just behind him, seeming to be lost in his thoughts. "Where's Ogden?"

Moon opened his mouth to answer but said nothing.

Brooks nodded in understanding. "Should we go back for him?" Brooks asked. Abigail looked hopeful but that dropped before Moon answered.

"He wanted to stay. I don't think he wanted anybody to wonder about him."

"That sounds like him," Abigail answered. Her mouth smiled, but her eyes did not.

Brooks nodded again. "We have the lieutenant and his man, Barnett, in the wagon. I'm going to have one of our guys take him back to the railroad office. See if they have family. Something. Let them give them both their final arrangements."

"Seems fitting," Moon answered. He was not sure if it was, he just was not interested in such things. So far as he would ever be concerned, only Josiah and that creature got the fitting 'arrangement.' Josiah would stay in that cave, for however long, and nature would do whatever it would do. The creature was now nothing more than ash, blowing in the Arizona wind.

"I'll go with," Decuir offered. "In case there's questions."

Moon sighed bitterly. "What will you tell them?"

Abigail thought for a moment. She looked to the wagon, to the distant tents at the end of town, where everybody comes in the first time. She considered her saloon, the many camps before, and the many that would follow. It would all happen again. There would be more people, an endless, uncountable more. But none would be Moon. None would be the measure of Lieutenant Harris.

They would never again be Josiah Ogden.

"As I see it," Abigail finally answered, "you can tell them the truth or lie. It doesn't matter. Who would believe this story?"

Historical Note

Work commenced on the Cañon Diablo Bridge on January 18, 1882, and the bridge opened for business, as scheduled, beginning on July 1, 1882. The rail line continued construction and would link up with the Southern Pacific Railroad in California by August of 1883.

Within ten years of the original bridge construction, a Navajo trading post was the only remaining structure. It burned down in the 1930's. The town adopted the English spelling of Canyon Diablo at the turn of the century and it lingered painfully for years. Today, only a few low stone walls remain to identify the town.

As early as 1900, the bridge has continued to be replaced and improved throughout its history. The bridge is still in operation today.

Little records exist of the town once known as Cañon Diablo and much of what is reported has questionable historical authenticity.

None of the surviving historical records or accounts mentions any attack by a monster.

About the Author

Jason McCord is a writer, editor, and frequent convention panelist. He was accidentally given a love for the macabre at an early age, and a fondness for westerns much later. He has lived in Arizona for most of his life and continues to out of habit.